The Secret of Sanctuary Island

Together the two of them looked around the room. The left wall had an opening leading into the breakfast area. Across the room, there was a huge red brick fireplace. Suddenly Todd felt Kevin's cold and clammy hand on his arm. He followed Kevin's gaze to the right. An entertainment center covered most of the wall. Three slots were open, one above the television and two between the speakers. Black wires hung limp, waiting to be attached somewhere.

"You were right about this guy," said Kevin.

Todd nodded his head slowly. "But how are we going to prove it?"

The Secret of

Sanctuary Island

A. M. MONSON

Beech Tree Books New York

Printed in the United States of America.
First Beech Tree Edition, 1992. 1 2 3 4 5 6 7 8 9 10
Library of Congress Cataloging in Publication Data
Monson, Ann M. The Secret of Sanctuary Island / by Ann M. Monson p. cm.
Summary: While still becoming accustomed to his father's remarriage, thirteen-year-old Todd and a friend set out to prove they observed a burglary no one believes happened.
[1. Mystery and detective stories. 1. Stepmothers—Fiction.]
ISBN 0-688-11693-0 1. Title. PZ7.M7628Hc 1991 [Fic]—dc20
90-6479 CIP AC

For Marie, Darlene, Pip, and Luanne,
your support helped
make the dream come true.

ACKNOWLEDGMENTS

Thank you Susan Pearson for your thorough and candid remarks. They helped toughen this writer's skin.

Thanks also go to Larry Gabrick, Janann Sims, and Officer Mary Ketzner. Your areas of expertise were invaluable.

The Secret of Sanctuary Island

Chapter One

As Todd turned the corner of Windom Avenue, he spotted the basketball hoop in his driveway. He shifted the schoolbooks to his left hand. Dribbling an imaginary ball with his right hand, he dodged a rosebush in Old Man Pritchard's yard. One stride away from the basket, he leaped into the air. In his mind, he saw the ball roll around the rim once, then drop through the hoop. The soles of his high tops hit the concrete with a loud thump. He tossed the books onto his father's mud-splattered Chevy.

Two wooden braces on the back wall of the garage supported a canoe. He lifted the tarp, folding it neatly as he stepped backward. Soon the entire seventeen feet of the sleek canoe was exposed. Todd ran his palm along its smooth, cool surface. With the knuckles of his other hand, he made a gentle rapping sound. He smiled. No more pretending he heard waves lapping against the side of the canoe. Tonight he and Kevin would hear real waves. He grabbed his books and hurried into the house.

"I've been waiting for you," said Dad, without turning around.

Todd plopped his books onto the kitchen counter and leaned on them. His father remained quiet as he concentrated on pouring coffee into the steel thermos. Already his muscular arms were turning a bronze color from the growing hours of sunshine. He wasn't a tall man, barely five feet seven inches. Todd hoped he would grow to be that tall, even taller. The combination of the blondness he'd inherited from his mother and his shortness always prompted people to treat him as if he were two years younger than he really was.

"How much longer will you have to work second shift?" Todd asked.

"If we don't get too many rainy days, we should be done with the freeway by July first."

Oh, no, thought Todd. Two more months of eating dinner with Jan and answering her endless questions. How was school today? Did he like basketball? Would he like to be on a team? He felt like the frog they had dissected in science class.

"Remember our talk a couple of weeks ago?" Dad turned to face him.

"Sure," answered Todd. He'd promised to tell Jan more about his comings and goings.

"Yesterday I asked you to leave a note letting her know where you were and when you'd be home."

"I forgot," muttered Todd. He bent the corner of his English book.

"Well, your forgetting caused a lot of unnecessary worry on her part."

"But I told *you*," insisted Todd. The disappointed look on his father's face made him wish he could take the words back.

"That's not the point," said Dad. "You know she can't reach me at the road site unless it's an emergency."

Geez! Why did Jan have to make such a big deal about everything? He'd only been at Kevin's house. He'd stayed for dinner, then they'd watched a documentary for history class.

"I'll try to remember to leave a note." Todd knew his father expected a response.

"Good," said Dad. "Because if you don't prove yourself responsible enough to start communicating with Jan, then I will think you are not responsible enough to take the canoe out."

"What?" Todd jerked his head up.

"It's up to you." Dad began packing his dinner into a small cooler.

Todd shoved the books away from him. He wouldn't be having this problem if Dad hadn't remarried. All of a sudden the rules had changed. Instead of reporting to one person, now he had to tell two people. It wasn't fair. "You'll get used to her," his mother had told him. "You might even end up liking her." Todd straightened and rubbed his forehead. It wasn't that he disliked her, exactly. She just wasn't part of his life. She was an outsider.

"I know it's been hard these past three months," said his father, breaking into his thoughts. "Our marriage has meant a lot of changes for you. But just give Jan a chance." He reached on top of the refrigerator for his hard hat. "Come on, I'll help you with the canoe."

They went into the garage. Todd lifted the two-wheeled cart, with its canvas platform, off the wall and set it on the concrete. Meanwhile his father placed the cooler and thermos on the Chevy's hood. Todd watched as he ducked under the canoe's center thwart. Using his shoulders, he lifted the canoe into the air. After a few steps, he stood next to the cart and in one fluid motion, he pushed the canoe off his shoulders, turned it right side up, and lowered it onto the waiting platform.

Todd grabbed an orange bungee cord and hooked one end to the canvas frame, then handed his father the other end. It stretched over the gunwales, holding the canoe to the platform. If the canoe's weight was not distributed evenly, sometimes the wheels would roll. This might send either the stern or the bow crashing to the concrete. To prevent this, Dad gently lowered the bow until it touched the garage floor.

"Sure is a beauty," said Dad. He ran his hand along the wooden gunwale. "When school lets out, you and I will have to go out one afternoon." He winked at Todd. "Can't let you have all the fun."

Todd knew his father was envious of him and Kevin taking the canoe out on such a beautiful May afternoon. He and Dad had just bought it late last fall and had made it out only once before the lakes froze.

Dad opened the car door and laid the cooler and thermos on the front seat. "Remember, you have to wear your life preservers tonight." Todd nodded. "Make sure you're home no later than nine-fifteen, and, most important, be careful. Don't get cocky out there. The ice has been gone only three weeks, and that water is still dangerously cold."

"We'll be careful," replied Todd.

Dad nodded, then sat down in the driver's seat. Todd watched him back the car down the driveway and into the street. After waving, he hurried into the house. Kevin would be here any minute, and he needed to change into his old tennis shoes. The white high tops with their fluorescent orange laces were brand new and he didn't want to get them wet. On his way upstairs, he wondered where his tackle box was. A few minutes later he rushed down the steps as the doorbell rang.

"Hi," said Kevin as Todd opened the door. "You ready?"

"Just about," answered Todd. Kevin followed him into the kitchen. He leaned his fishing pole against the cupboard and began looking around.

Todd recognized the expression. "Hungry?"

"Starved!" answered Kevin. "Ever since my mom put us on that diet, the most I get after school is an apple."

Todd opened the door to the refrigerator. On the top shelf lay a bag with a note attached.

"I made you some sandwiches. Have a good time. Jan."

Todd handed Kevin a box of doughnuts and a quart of milk, then peeked into the bag. Bean sprouts poked at the plastic wrap. It had to be one of her vegetarian specialties. Better not leave them here—she might say something to Dad. He'd have to take them along and get rid of them later.

He made two new peanut butter sandwiches and dropped them into the bag along with a couple of doughnuts. Quickly he rummaged through the drawer for paper and a pencil.

"Went with Kevin. Be back at 9:15. Todd."

Jan knew about their outing tonight, but he wasn't taking any chances.

Kevin grabbed another doughnut, then they headed for the garage.

"I've never seen a fiberglass canoe before," said Kevin, pushing on the cane seat with his thumb.

"Fastest lake canoe made," said Todd proudly. He carefully laid life preservers, paddles, and Kevin's fishing pole on the bottom. Searching the corner of the garage, he found his pole and miniature tackle box. After laying them in the canoe, he picked up the bow. "You hold onto the stern, and we'll wheel it down to the lake."

"How come we have to use the cart?" asked Kevin. "Why don't we just carry it?"

"I think my dad's afraid we'll drop it or something."

They walked the three blocks to the lake and waited for the cars to pass on Lakewood Drive.

After crossing, they had to stop again for two roller skaters on the bike path.

"How about here?" asked Kevin, when they reached the water.

"Too rocky," answered Todd. He didn't want to be the first one to put a scratch in the canoe's shiny finish. They continued on until he found a sandier spot.

"This is good," said Todd.

A passing train on the south end of the lake blew its whistle.

"Hang onto the stern," called Todd, as he let go of the bow. It dropped to the ground.

He glared at Kevin. "I told you to hang onto the stern."

"I didn't hear you," said Kevin. He cocked his head to one side and narrowed his eyes. "You sure are touchy about this canoe."

"I just don't want anything to happen to it, okay?" He unhooked the bungee cord, then picked up a life preserver. "Here, put this on." Kevin hesitated. "I promised we'd wear them." Reluctantly, Kevin fastened the straps.

Next he helped Todd lift the canoe off the cart. "Boy, is this light."

"Of course," said Todd. "It's an ultralight."

He picked up the cart and laid it in the canoe. Then he pushed the bow into the water and motioned for Kevin to get in. The canoe wobbled as Kevin stumbled over the cart. When he was settled in the bow, Todd shoved the canoe into the water and jumped into the stern. His right tennis shoe skimmed the lake's surface. Dad was right, it was cold.

He had forgotten how easily and quickly the canoe sliced through water. They reached Sanctuary Island in fifteen minutes and began casting toward shore. Ten minutes later, Kevin was wrapping his hand around a third tiny sunfish, while Todd had missed a couple of bites. He really wasn't in the mood to catch fish anyway. It was more fun dipping his paddle into the water and seeing how the canoe reacted.

"Let's try a different spot," said Kevin. "They're too small here."

"Okay," said Todd. He reeled his line in and they paddled around to the other side of the island. They stopped twenty feet out. A sign on shore read: WILDLIFE REFUGE, LANDING IS PRO-

HIBITED. Todd watched a white egret fly overhead and land in the top of a tree.

"They're still too small," complained Kevin, slipping a sunfish back into the water. "Let's go somewhere else."

Todd had an idea. "Why don't we go over to Balsam and fish along that rocky shoreline near the railroad bridge?"

"That's a lot of paddling," said Kevin.

"I hear the sunfish are bigger," said Todd, trying to make it sound as tempting as possible.

Kevin reeled in his line. "Let's go."

Todd smiled. He knew his friend would agree to go. Kevin was always on the lookout for big fish. His grandfather had told him stories about sunfish the size of dinner plates and forty-pound northerns that could leap over a fishing boat. After seeing how tiny the sunfish were in Alpine, Todd had decided that the stories were just that—stories. He looked at his watch; it was almost six-thirty.

They paddled under the Lakewood Drive bridge and entered the half-mile-long channel connecting Alpine to Balsam. On the right near the shoreline, an adult Canadian goose followed by five fuzzy goslings and another adult swam in a straight line. They were headed toward Alpine. Probably going to the island for the night, thought Todd. They always did.

On the left was Travers Road. It followed the channel for a block, then wound its way through six blocks of houses before it reached the southern end of Balsam Lake.

"This canoe sure moves a lot faster than aluminum canoes," said Kevin, turning around.

"Costs a lot more, too," said Todd. "My dad saved two years for it." He scanned the shiny wood of the center thwart and the thousands of tiny squares beneath his feet. The canoe was made of layers of cloth soaked in resin, he remembered the salesman saying. Todd found it hard to imagine pieces of cloth being turned into a canoe; it was easier to think of it as sort of a waterproof carpet.

The channel narrowed and trees lined the banks. Up ahead a railroad bridge crossed the channel, its black creosote timbers creating shadows. Todd always got an eerie feeling when he passed through this area. It would be perfect for a scene in a horror movie, especially later in the summer when the slimy green algae took over the water.

He could see the horror movie opening with a scene of two people gliding along in a canoe. Suddenly their paddles are sucked beneath the surface. Next the canoe begins to slowly sink into the green slime. The canoeists scream and try to climb the timbers. The algae sends out tentacles that wrap around their feet and knees.

On Todd's left a loud splash broke the quiet.

"What was that?" asked Kevin.

"Probably just a carp flipping its tail," answered Todd. He certainly wasn't going to admit he'd jumped at the sound, too.

When they entered Balsam, Todd could feel the cool breeze off the water, and the sun in the west caused him to squint. To the north, clouds were beginning to move in.

They headed for the opposite shore. Thirty feet from the rocky shoreline, Todd stopped paddling. He checked his watch; it was almost seven-fifteen.

"We'll have to leave at eight-thirty to make it back on time," he said. Kevin nodded his head and cast toward shore. Todd could tell he was only half listening. It was going to be up to him to keep an eye on the time. He didn't want anything to ruin his chances of using the canoe again.

Chapter Two

Between casts, Todd looked around the lake. Of the three lakes in Hidden Springs, Balsam was his favorite. It wasn't surrounded with houses like Alpine. Only in the southeast corner, where Travers Road crossed the railroad tracks, were the houses visible. From the canoe, Todd could see the last of the sun's rays reflecting off their windows. The rest of the east side was swamp, with only the entrance to the channel interrupting the small trees and cattails.

On the north end, a steep bank led to another set of railroad tracks. All the rail lines reminded Todd of his bike wheel. Like spokes heading toward an axle, the tracks passed through the suburb of Hidden Springs on their way to the main train yard in Minneapolis.

In front of him, park area ran the entire length of the west side. As at Alpine, there was a walking path closer to the lake and a bike path near Travers Road. The best part about the west side was the trees. Huge old elms and hundreds of smaller trees kept anyone on the lake from seeing the road and houses beyond it. On a quiet night like this, Todd could imagine himself in the wild. He was a French explorer paddling his way down the St. Lawrence Seaway, or a trapper floating downstream to the nearest trading post.

He reeled in his line, decided on a different spot, then cast the plastic silver minnow toward it. The bobber drifted on the surface for a few seconds. Suddenly it was yanked underneath. Out of reflex, Todd set the hook.

"Kevin!" he breathed. Todd didn't know what he had caught, but it felt like a torpedo gone haywire.

"Wow!" said Kevin. "Your pole's bent in half. You must have a monster on there. Don't lose him."

"I'm trying not to," sputtered Todd. He gripped the rod tighter. His pulse raced as he fought the big fish.

The pole snapped into a straight line and the bobber danced on the surface. Todd lost his balance and struggled to quiet the rocking canoe before reeling in. Below the bobber the line had either broken or been bitten. His weighted silver minnow was gone.

"I—I bet that was a fifteen-pound northern," he said, his pulse starting to return to normal.

"Or a record-breaking walleye," said Kevin. "Geez, I wish you'd gotten that fish! We could have showed it to my brother, Sam. Bet that would get his attention away from that junker car he's always working on."

"We couldn't have kept it," said Todd, fighting his growing disappointment. "It's still two and a half weeks before the season opens." His dad was a firm believer in following the Department of Natural Resources' rules. If he ever found out they had kept a fish out of season, the canoe wouldn't be the only thing taken away.

"Boy, watching you sure made me hungry," said Kevin. He reached for the bag of sandwiches.

Water that had dripped from their paddles when switching sides had soaked into the bag. It tore as Kevin pulled on it.

"What's this?" asked Kevin, eyeing one of the sandwiches.

"Jan made it," answered Todd. "Looks like bean sprouts and lettuce. There's probably cucumber and yogurt dressing in there, too."

Kevin wrinkled his nose. "God, no wonder you're skinny." He grabbed another sandwich. "Think I'll stick to peanut butter."

Todd hated being small. Not only were all the boys in seventh grade bigger than he was, the girls were, too. If only he were a little taller. "Don't worry," Dad had told him. "If you're like me you'll start filling out when you turn fifteen." That was still two years away. He let out a sigh and looked around the lake.

The pinkness from the setting sun had been replaced by a thick blanket of gray clouds. He glanced at his watch; it was eight-fifteen. No use rigging up his line again. They'd be leaving in a few minutes.

He spotted a canoe making its way along the northeast corner of the lake. "That's funny," said Todd. Kevin turned around, and Todd pointed at the canoe.

"Just two guys out canoeing," he mumbled, his mouth full.

"But look how close they're paddling to shore, and the one in the stern keeps looking over his left shoulder."

"So what?" asked Kevin.

"It's weird," said Todd, and he continued to watch. When the canoe reached the point closest to them, Todd waved and called, "Hello!"

Neither man answered. The one in the stern pulled his black baseball cap farther down on his forehead and looked straight ahead. The one in the bow, with the red hair and beard, looked toward shore. Both wore dark shirts and no life preservers.

"Friendly, aren't they?" said Todd. Most canoeists would say hi or at least wave. He watched the canoe disappear.

"Hey, where'd they go?" asked Kevin.

"Into Juniper Lake," answered Todd. "The railroad tracks run over a concrete tunnel that connects the two lakes." Todd didn't like Juniper. It was a small lake with lots of algae growth. Later in the summer, it would smell.

"Let's go in there," said Kevin. "I've never seen it."

Todd looked at his watch; it was twenty after eight. They still had ten minutes before they had to start back. Besides, he was curious about what those two guys were up to. "Okay," agreed Todd.

He hadn't seen any fishing poles, but they could have been lying on the bottom of the canoe. But why come out so late? It was almost dark, and you couldn't keep anything except panfish. Maybe they were going after game fish like the one he had earlier. If that was the case, they'd be poaching.

"This is great," said Kevin, as they approached the concrete archway. "Look at the graffiti. 'Jeanne R. loves Brad P.' 'Mr. Jensen sucks raw eggs.' "

Todd carefully guided the canoe down the middle of the channel. There was less than eighteen inches of clearance on either side. Trying to read more graffiti, Kevin twisted and turned in his seat. The gunwale inched toward the concrete.

"Kevin!" snapped Todd. His voice bounced off the walls. He snatched his paddle out of the water and used the end of the blade to push the canoe away from the tunnel's rough surface.

"Okay, okay," said Kevin. He returned his paddle to the water.

Todd breathed a sigh of relief when they cleared the second archway.

"I didn't expect the lake to be this small," said Kevin, looking around. He leaned over the side and touched the bottom with his paddle. "Or this shallow," he continued. To keep the canoe balanced, Todd leaned the opposite way.

Across the lake from them, Todd saw the canoe pulled up on shore. A nearby path lead into the trees. There goes my poaching theory, they're probably just visiting someone, Todd thought. When he looked up into the trees, he could barely see the outline of a roof and chimney.

Thinking it was time to head back, he glanced at his watch; it was eight-thirty-five. He was just about to say, "Let's go," when the two men appeared on the path. They were both carrying something.

Todd squinted. The man wearing the baseball cap carried what looked like a stereo receiver. On top of that was a wooden box the same size and shape as the receiver. It was similar to the box his mother stored the good silverware in. The other man, the one with the beard, held two smaller things. A VCR and a compact disc player? But why . . . ? Todd swallowed. They were watching a robbery!

"Let's get out of here," he whispered through dry lips. Kevin nodded.

Todd reached for his paddle. It slipped from his knees and banged against the wooden gunwale. The sound echoed around the quiet lake. The two men jerked their heads up. Quickly they laid everything in the canoe, then shoved it into the water.

Todd froze. Were the men coming after them? Yes! his instinct shouted. He grabbed the paddle and thrust the blade into the water. Using sweep strokes, he turned the canoe around.

Kevin's frenzied paddling in the tunnel made it impossible for Todd to steer and paddle at the same time. He turned the handle and used the blade as a rudder, trying to keep them from banging into the wall and losing time.

"Come on!" muttered Todd, as he waited for the concrete to end. Just before they left the tunnel, he glanced over his shoulder. The men were halfway across Juniper. Todd stabbed at the water with his paddle.

If they were caught, the two men could knock them unconscious—even drown them! Todd shuddered at the vision of them floating in the water like bloated dead fish. Todd tried paddling faster, but soon his shoulders ached and his hands throbbed from clutching the paddle so hard. He stole another look back. The canoe shot from the tunnel.

"They're gaining on us," he yelled. Kevin didn't answer. He paddled frantically, sending water flying toward Todd.

He peered into the gray of oncoming darkness. To their left, a steep bank led to the railroad tracks, and beyond that there was another hill. It was their only chance. On land they could hide or split up and run. Out here they were easy prey, too easy.

Using a cross between a forward stroke and a sweep stroke, he aimed the canoe north. The bow raced toward shore. Todd tried to soften the impact by back-paddling. It wasn't enough. The bow slammed into the rocks, sending him to his knees. The canoe turned on its side as the two boys stumbled into the lake. Water soaked into Todd's jeans, weighing him down as he waded toward shore.

Kevin, ten feet ahead, clawed his way up the hill. Todd yanked on the bow, pulling some of the canoe onto the rocks, then he raced after Kevin. When they reached the top, knee-high grass, brush, and tree branches closed behind them. They tripped over blackened railroad ties.

"Forget them," said a harsh voice. Todd stopped in his tracks. "Get the canoe."

"Kevin!" Todd whispered, as loud as he dared.

Dropping to his hands and knees, he crawled back to the edge of the hill.

Parting the brush with his hands, he peered into the darkness below. He could barely see the outline of the two canoes. A loud scraping noise filled his ears. His hold tightened and a twig snapped under the pressure.

Kevin, his breathing heavy, crawled alongside him. Todd motioned to him not to speak, then turned his attention back to the canoes. He heard two paddles in the water. Were they taking the canoe? He began to panic.

"We'll dump everything into the lake, then swamp the canoe."

"Thank God!" breathed Todd. They weren't stealing the canoe.

The water came alive as poles, paddles, and tackle tumbled into the blackness. Todd heard a final splash as the cart fell into the water, then a giant whoosh as the two men forced the gunwale beneath the lake's surface.

"That'll teach those snoopy kids," said a second voice.

The water swirled and gurgled as the two

paddles finished their strokes. Todd stood up and tried to follow the canoe with his eyes, but it was too dark. The sound grew fainter. Finally he no longer heard it.

"What do we do now?" asked Kevin. He raced down the hill after Todd.

"We get the canoe," answered Todd. Forty feet away, the canoe's gunwales floated above the water.

"Are you crazy?" replied Kevin. "That water is freezing!"

"I'm not going home without the canoe," said Todd, stepping out of his wet jeans. "See if the paddles have floated into shore." He dropped the wet denim and life preserver in a heap, then stepped into the icy water. His foot slipped on an algae-covered rock, and he plunged into the freezing darkness. The cold forced his breath out in gasps. Trying to warm himself, he stroked and stroked. Finally the initial shock lessened, and he swam to the canoe.

When he reached it, he swung his left hand up and held onto the gunwale. His cheek rested against the hull while he caught his breath. The canoe was full of water up to three inches below the gunwale. It would take forever to climb inside and paddle toward shore with his hands. The quickest way was to pull it in. With his right hand, he searched for the tie-off rope. Even in the frigid water, he could feel the deep scratches in the hull. His shivering worsened. "Where is it?" he muttered. Finally he located it and grabbed the rope with his left hand. He kicked his feet in unison, stroked with his right arm, then pulled on the tie-off rope. Over and over he stroked and tugged, slowly inching his way toward shore.

Ten feet from land, the muscles in his legs began to weaken and he no longer felt his left arm. He thought his foot touched a rock. Was he imagining it? Kevin came splashing into the water, and Todd felt him helping with the canoe. Together they pulled and tipped it at the same time. Water poured back into the lake.

"I found the paddles," said Kevin.

"Go-oo-od," said Todd, his teeth chattering uncontrollably. The area between his shoulder blades ached from shivering.

"Here," said Kevin, removing his life jacket and sweatshirt. "Put this on." He handed his sweatshirt over.

"Th-th-an-ks," said Todd. He took off his wet shirt, put on Kevin's dry one, then refastened his life preserver. After Todd pulled on his wet jeans, the two of them climbed into the canoe. Still trembling from the cold water, he checked his watch; the crystal was broken. They were going to be late, but at least they had the canoe.

Chapter Three

Todd held his breath as they approached the railroad bridge over the channel. If the two men were waiting to ambush them, this would be the spot. He stopped paddling and listened. The sound from Kevin's paddle joined the cricket chirps and bullfrog blasts. Hearing nothing out of the ordinary, Todd returned the blade to the water.

A few minutes later they passed under the Lakewood Drive bridge and entered Alpine. All was quiet except for the honking sounds coming from Sanctuary Island. The geese were angry at something. Todd's wet jeans trapped the cold next to his body, and he continued to shiver. A single banging sound echoed across the lake, then one by one the geese quieted.

Todd guided the canoe to the same spot where they had launched. "Let's turn it over," he said, climbing out.

Water gurgled onto the ground. The sound reminded him of a garden hose left running. It's too much water, he thought. He walked to the bow and ran his fingers over the hull. Todd winced when he felt the deep gouges. Slowly he moved his hand downward toward the gunwale. Eight inches later, he came across a crooked vertical line. Using his fingertips he gently began to apply pressure. Suddenly the material gave way.

"Shit!"

"What?" asked Kevin.

"We put a hole in it," answered Todd.

"When?"

"It must've happened when we hit the rocks on Balsam. We hit pretty hard." He shook his head. "Damn those two guys. We'll keep it upside down and carry it home. You put the bow on your right shoulder, and I'll put the stern on my left." After positioning the canoe, each of them knelt down and picked up a paddle.

"Scratches and a hole," muttered Todd as they walked. "Geez, what will Dad say?"

Maybe he could take the fifty dollars he had in the bank and have it fixed. What if it cost more? What if it cost a hundred or five hundred dollars? On his allowance, it would take forever to save five hundred dollars.

As they turned the corner of Windom Avenue, Todd spotted his house. The garage security light was on, and a baby-blue squad car sat in the driveway.

She'd called the cops! Todd couldn't believe it! He gritted his teeth. All kids were late sometimes. Why did Jan have to turn it into a big deal? Why couldn't she have just waited?

"Now we can tell the police what we saw," said Kevin.

Grudgingly, Todd admitted Kevin was right. They would have to talk to the police sometime.

When they reached the edge of the lawn, he

saw two officers and Jan walking to the car. The shorter officer pointed in their direction. Jan came running toward them.

"You two had me scared to death!" She helped them lay the canoe down, then put a hand on each of their shoulders. Quickly she steered them toward the house.

"But we need to tell the police something," said Todd, trying to escape her grasp.

"That can wait a couple of minutes," Jan said firmly. "First we're going to get you out of those wet clothes."

"We'll come in," said one of the officers.

When they reached the linen closet, Jan stopped and reached inside. "Wrap yourselves in these," she said, handing them each a blanket. "Then come back into the dining room. Kevin, I'm going to call your mother and tell her you're all right."

In the bathroom, Todd removed his jeans and Kevin's sweatshirt. "Here," Todd said, handing it to him. He wrapped himself in the blanket. It felt warm against his cold, damp legs.

Kevin pulled the sweatshirt over his head, removed his wet jeans, then wrapped the blanket around his waist. They went and sat down at the dining room table.

"I'm Officer Helgstrom and this is my partner, Officer Grady," said the policewoman. "You two had your parents very worried."

Jan entered the room. "Your mother is coming over to get you," she said to Kevin on her way to the kitchen.

"Looks to me like you swamped the canoe," said Officer Grady. He hooked the thumbs of his huge hands into his wide black leather belt.

Todd disliked him immediately.

"Well?" Grady stepped closer, towering over the boys.

"We didn't tip over," said Todd. "Two men chased us, and they swamped the canoe."

"Why did they chase you?" asked Helgstrom, taking a notepad from her hip pocket.

"We saw them robbing a place over on Juniper Lake," said Todd. Before he could continue the microwave buzzed. Jan removed two steaming mugs, stirred a packet of hot chocolate into each, then brought them to the table. Todd wrapped his hands around the outside and let the warmth seep into his fingers.

"What time was this possible robbery or burglary?" asked the female officer.

Todd was confused. "What's the difference?"

"If there is no one present," explained Helgstrom, "what you saw would be classified as a burglary."

Todd glanced at the clock; it was a little after eleven. "Two and a half hours ago," he answered. He took a sip of hot chocolate. The warm liquid felt good sliding down his throat.

"We haven't received any reports of a burglary," said Grady. He bent at the waist and put one hand on the table and the other on the back of Todd's chair.

His face was so close that Todd could see the individual hairs in his nose and smell the garlic on his breath.

"Maybe the people who were robbed aren't home yet," suggested Kevin.

Grady straightened and took a step backward. Todd breathed again and shot Kevin a grateful look.

"That's possible," said Officer Helgstrom. "Why don't you give us a description?"

"The one in the stern had black hair and wore

a dark-colored baseball cap and shirt," said Todd.

"What about the other one?" she asked.

"He had reddish hair and a beard," answered Kevin. "He wore a dark shirt, too."

"What kind of canoe?"

"Aluminum," answered Todd. He was finally starting to feel warm.

"Any identifying marks or numbers?"

Todd looked at Kevin. His friend shrugged his shoulders. "We didn't see any dents or anything," said Todd. "We weren't close enough to read watercraft numbers."

Officer Grady snorted. "Now, isn't that convenient?"

"What did they steal?" asked Officer Helgstrom.

"A stereo receiver and I think a box with good silverware inside," replied Todd.

"You think?" Grady leaned toward him again.

"It was almost dark," said Todd. He was getting angry. Grady was making him feel like he was the one who had done something wrong. "It looked like the kind of box my mother stores her good silverware in."

"Did they steal anything else?" she asked.

"The one with the beard carried two smaller things," said Kevin. "A CD player and a VCR?" He looked at Todd.

"That's what I saw, too." The blanket slipped from his shoulder, and he hurried to pull it back up. He saw Kevin smile at his embarrassment.

"You said you were chased." Helgstrom put the pen to her lips.

"From Juniper into Balsam," said Kevin.

"To the north end of Balsam," added Todd. "We landed and ran up the hill to the railroad tracks. They pulled our canoe back into the water, dumped everything into the lake, then swamped it." This last part he directed to Grady.

"Okay," said Officer Helgstrom. She put the notepad back into her pocket. "We'll go over and take a look. If we find something or if someone calls in a burglary we'll be back to talk to you." Jan followed them out the door.

If someone calls? Todd repeated the words in his mind. Why wouldn't they call? Officer Grady's voice caught his attention, and he padded over to the screen door.

"Stories—lots of kids—a good scare." Those

were the pieces of Grady's sentence he could hear. Opening the door, he peeked through the crack. The three of them were standing by the car. He thought he heard Jan say "Thanks," but he wasn't sure. The two officers got into the car and the engine roared to life. Quickly he closed the door and hurried back to his chair. Kevin started to ask what he had heard. Todd nodded toward the door. Jan entered the kitchen a second later.

"Do you have anything to eat?" asked Kevin.

Todd smiled. Good thing he could count on Kevin to think of their stomachs. He hadn't realized how hungry he was until now.

"Sure," answered Jan. She took out a box of granola bars and placed them on the table, then she made two more cups of hot chocolate.

Todd tore the wrapper off and took a bite. Jan's sandwiches would be sitting on the lake bottom. Would fish eat bean sprouts? Not if they were smart, they wouldn't.

There was a knock at the front door and Jan went to open it. Mrs. Jarvis stepped inside, her plump body filling the entryway. Kevin rose from his chair.

"Just a second," said Jan, and she disappeared into the bathroom. When she returned, she was carrying Kevin's pants. He looked at the blanket, then at the crumpled jeans.

"You can return the blanket later," said Jan.

Todd smiled when he saw the look of relief pass over his friend's face. He knew Kevin had thought she wanted him to change right there. At least he wasn't the only one who got embarrassed.

He wondered what Mrs. Jarvis would say to Kevin on the way home. His own mom would hug him first, then yell for two minutes and hug him again. Too bad she wasn't in town, thought Todd. She was in San Diego getting her R.N. certification at a school that offered an accelerated program. It'd be the middle of June before he would be able to see her. Would Dad call and tell her what happened?

He panicked. "Did you call Dad?"

"No," answered Jan. "I was going to wait until after the police had looked around the lakes for you. Turns out, on their way over here to answer the call, they flashed their spotlight on Alpine."

Whew! He leaned back in his chair. No use worrying Dad when he was all right. Well, almost all right. He'd just been scared. Tipping the mug up, he drank the last drop of hot chocolate.

"Why don't you take a hot shower, then go to bed," said Jan, clearing the table.

"I have to take care of the canoe first," said Todd stubbornly.

"I'll put the canoe on the rack." He looked at her. "Don't worry. I won't scratch it or drop it. I'll treat it as if it were my very own."

She probably couldn't do any more damage than what was already there, he decided. "Okay, but I *am* going to stay up and tell Dad what happened."

"He won't be home until one-thirty," snapped Jan. She put the mugs down and took a breath. "You can explain tomorrow," she said evenly.

Todd was too tired to argue with her. He would go upstairs and stay awake until Dad came home. Jan disappeared out the kitchen door, and he went to the living room window to watch. In two moves, she hoisted the canoe onto her shoulders. When he could no longer see her, he listened. He didn't hear any bumping or crashing noises, so he assumed it was safe to take a shower.

The warm water soothed the sore muscles in his arms and between his shoulder blades. After drying off he climbed into bed. He looked at the clock; it was almost midnight. Another hour and a half to wait. His eyelids felt heavy, and he rubbed them with his palms.

He had to stay awake and tell Dad what happened. Jan might tell him the wrong things or say it was his fault that they were late.

His eyelids shut. He snapped them open. Furiously he blinked his eyelids, but each time they stayed shut longer and longer. He decided to close his eyes for just a couple of minutes. That couldn't hurt anything. His breathing slowed, and he drifted off into an exhausted sleep.

Chapter Four

When Todd opened his eyes, he was lying on his stomach facing the digital clock. The second zero on twelve o'clock changed to a one. Sure was light for midnight, drifted through his mind. Midnight? He rolled over and sat up.

"Oh, great!" he muttered, as he scrambled out of bed. He jumped into a pair of sweatpants, then reached for a T-shirt. "Agh!" The muscles in his arms and back screamed at the upward movement. He couldn't remember ever being this sore.

The aroma of coffee greeted him when he opened the door. At least Dad was up. Now he had to find out how much Jan had told him. When he reached the dining room, his father was sitting at the table, the Saturday paper spread before him.

"Thought you were going to sleep all day," he said, raising his head. "Sit down. I'll make you some breakfast."

"Where's Jan?" asked Todd. Her purse wasn't in the usual spot on the counter.

"She had a house to show," answered Dad. He cracked a couple of eggs open, then whipped them with a fork.

Good, he thought. She wouldn't be there to interrupt him.

"As a matter of fact," he continued, "she's showing a house over by Juniper Lake."

Todd swallowed. "How much did she tell you?"

"As much as she could," answered Dad. He poured the eggs into the frypan and stirred in pieces of sausage.

Usually Todd inhaled whatever his dad cooked, but the thought of telling him about the canoe was making his stomach queasy. "There's a hole in the bow," he said quietly.

His father stopped stirring.

"I think it happened when we hit the rocks on Balsam. They were close to catching us. I tried to back-paddle. . . ."

Dad put his hand up. "We'll get it fixed." He removed the frypan from the stove and pushed the scrambled eggs onto a plate. The food and a glass of milk appeared on the placemat in front of Todd.

"I called the police this morning," said Dad, sitting down.

Todd looked at him expectantly. Now he'd find out what had happened.

"They didn't receive a burglary call or find anything unusual when they investigated."

How could they not find anything? Todd poked at his eggs. It didn't make sense. "Which one did you talk to?"

"Officer Grady," he answered. "Does it matter?"

"The other one, Officer Helgstrom, seemed to believe us. Grady acted like we were making up a story."

"Were you?" asked Dad.

"No!" Todd pushed his plate away.

"It seems"—Dad straightened in the chair—"that the police get a lot of calls from worried parents about teenagers who are out on the lake at night. Often the reason they're late is that they've swamped the canoe or just fooled around too long. When they get home, they make up stories to avoid being punished."

So that's what Grady was telling Jan last night. That they were making up a story to cover themselves. Then she passed this on to Dad without giving him a chance to explain. His face grew hard. Leave it to Jan to turn the situation into a national crisis! What angered him even more was that Dad sounded like he believed her. He had to prove it wasn't a story. But how?

"Let's go over to Juniper," he blurted out.

"And do what?" asked Dad, setting his coffee cup down.

"I'll show you where the canoe landed. We can knock on people's doors. If someone is on vacation, that would explain why a burglary wasn't reported." He watched Dad tap his forefinger against the rim of the mug. At least he was thinking about it.

"All right," he said, after a few seconds. "But you'd better eat some breakfast first."

Todd pulled his plate back and ate. The eggs were cold, but he didn't care. Going over to Juniper would clear everything up. He was sure of it. After he gulped down the rest of his milk, they left.

Dad drove the three blocks to Alpine, then turned right onto one-way Lakewood Drive. People on bikes and roller blades raced around the path next to the road, while joggers and walkers used the path closer to the lake.

"Sure can tell it's a nice spring weekend, everybody's out." Dad tilted his head toward the lake.

They crossed over the channel and turned right on Travers Road. Todd noticed the geese were in the same area as last night. The adults and goslings plucked at the blades of green grass.

Travers Road turned away from the channel, and Todd lost sight of the geese. After a few blocks they crossed the railroad tracks at the southeast end of Balsam Lake. Two hundred yards down the rail line, there was an old wooden bridge. Dad had told him it gave the residents on Burnside Lane another way to get out besides Travers Road. It was also a shortcut to the north side of Alpine Lake. Todd knew because he had ridden his bike across it.

There was hardly anyone out biking or walking on the paths around Balsam. It wasn't as attractive as Alpine because the trails ended near the railroad tracks on the north end. Also, not as many people lived around Balsam. They traveled along the west side until they reached Twenty-first Street. Dad turned left and drove one block, then stopped the car. There were houses to the left and trees on the right.

"We should be able to get to the lake from here," said Dad, looking around. "The street up there on the right is Huron. It's the only one that would have a house that has direct access to Juniper Lake. If we go through these trees, we'll end up between the tunnel and Huron Street."

Todd closed the door behind him. After a hundred feet, the railroad tracks appeared, the same ones they had escaped to last night. He followed his dad over the loose gravel that lined the tracks. Again the elm trees shaded them. Raspberry stems with their newly sprouted leaves and sharp thorns snagged at Todd's sweatpants.

"Here we are," said Dad, when they reached the lake.

Todd glanced around. The tunnel was off to his right. To his left and down a block was the clearing where he'd seen the canoe pulled up. "This way."

Pushing, then holding the branches so they wouldn't snap back at Dad, he slowly made his way toward the open area. He was positive the canoe's keel mark and two sets of footprints would be in the sand. Dad would have to believe him then. He stepped into the clearing. It was almost fifteen feet wide. The canoe had been pulled up next to the birch tree on the other side.

"There should be a mark here," said Todd, kneeling down and inspecting the ground. But there was no mark and instead of two sets of footprints he found only one very soggy and water-filled set. The dampness soaked into the right knee area of his sweatpants.

"Did it rain last night?" asked Todd.

"I don't think so," answered Dad.

Why was the ground so wet, wondered Todd? He rose and investigated the other side of the clearing. It was bone dry.

"There's a house up the hill," said Dad, pointing.

Todd could see the white siding and part of a window. They headed toward it. The trees created an archway over them and a thick layer of woodchips covered the path. They wouldn't see any footprints in this, thought Todd. He kicked one of the larger pieces and watched it bounce off the path. When they reached the lawn, Todd started up the stone path that led to the house.

"I don't want to scare whoever lives there," said Dad. "Let's go around to the front and knock."

As they made their way along the tree-lined perimeter of the lawn, Todd studied the house. It was two stories high with a big picture window looking out over the backyard. Sliding glass doors opened onto a concrete-slab patio that ended just past a doorway leading into the garage. They continued alongside the building until they reached the driveway.

Todd surveyed the area. The railroad tracks would be to his left on the other side of the trees. Across Huron Street were three houses, all single-level rambler types. The farthest one had a FOR SALE sign stuck in the yard. Jan's gray Ford sat in the driveway.

There was only one house on the east side—the one they were standing in front of. "This has to be the house," said Todd. He looked at Dad. "The stone path leads right to their patio doors. Besides, if the burglars had crossed the street, wouldn't someone have seen them?"

"Possibly," said Dad. "Let's go find out." Todd pushed the doorbell. When he didn't hear anything, he pushed it again.

"I'm coming," said an irritated voice inside the house. The door swung open and a bald-headed man stood in the entryway. "Yes?"

"Hello," said Dad. "My name is John Benson and this is my son, Todd."

Todd smiled but the man ignored him. He sure was dressed up for a Saturday, thought Todd. His brown pants were neatly creased and his barrel-shaped chest was covered by a tan sweater.

"My son and a friend of his were out in the canoe last night when they witnessed two men coming down your path. They may have committed a burglary."

Todd lost his view of the hallway as the man slowly pulled the door tight to his body. "They took a VCR and a stereo receiver," said Todd. "They hopped into a canoe and chased us."

The man eyed him carefully. "You think they broke into my house? Nonsense!"

Todd felt his heart drop to his knees. "But the path leads right to your patio doors."

"They could have robbed one of the other houses," said the man, motioning across the street.

A door slammed in the house. The man turned his head slightly, then looked back at them impatiently.

"Now if you'll excuse me, my wife's not feeling well."

"Are you sure you're not missing a VCR or a CD player?" blurted Todd.

"Young man!" His sharp tone stopped Todd from saying anything else. "I would know if anything was missing."

"Sorry to have bothered you." Dad started down the steps.

"Good-bye," said the man, and he closed the door.

"Maybe he's right," said his father, as they headed toward the street. "Perhaps it was one of the other houses that was burglarized."

As they crossed the street, Todd hoped it was true. In the back of his mind, though, he doubted it was possible. The burglars hadn't been out of their sight long enough for them to come up the hill, cross the street, steal what they did, then make it back down to the canoe.

They stopped and asked a man who was mowing his yard. No, he shook his head. He hadn't been robbed or seen anything suspicious, but he'd keep his eyes open. Dad thanked him, and they went on to the second house. A woman opened the door, and they received the same response.

They walked up the last driveway, past Jan's

car, to the green rambler. A white-haired man in his late sixties opened the door. Todd could hear Jan's voice in the background.

"Hello, my name is John Benson, and this is my son, Todd."

"Nice to meet you," replied the man. He extended his hand. "Name's Burt Polaski." The two men exchanged handshakes.

"Todd and a friend of his believe they witnessed a burglary last night. Perhaps it was your house that was hit?"

Burt looked at Todd. "No." He shook his head. "We weren't robbed." He stroked his chin. "Can't say that I'm too surprised to hear of something like that happening though."

"What do you mean?" asked Dad.

"Well," Burt took a breath, "the three houses on this side, we're decent folk, watch out for one another, that kind of thing. But that house up there . . ." He pointed to the first house they had stopped at.

Todd felt his hopes rise.

"Unfriendly lot, they are. They've lived there three months, and none of us know who they are."

"What's the matter?" asked a gray-haired woman. She stepped into the doorway and stood next to Burt.

"This young man witnessed a burglary," answered her husband.

"Oh, my goodness!" she said. "You weren't hurt, were you?"

"No," answered Todd.

"That's good." She put her arm on Burt's. "See, I told you our neighborhood wouldn't be left unscathed. I'll be so glad when we move into a security building." She smiled at Todd and his dad. "Excuse me," and she disappeared into the house.

"She thinks we'll be safer," said Burt. "Actually"—he lowered his voice—"I'm looking forward to not having to shovel snow or mow the grass."

"I know what you mean," said Dad, chuckling, then he became serious. "Could we leave our phone number with you, in case you hear or see anything?"

"Why, certainly," said Burt. He stepped inside, then returned after a few seconds with a pencil and paper.

Dad wrote down the number and handed it back to him. "Don't hesitate to call."

"I won't," replied Burt. "Good-bye."

They turned and headed toward the driveway. Todd was silent as he followed his father up the street, past the two-story white house. When they reached the railroad tracks, Jan's car sped by them.

"She doesn't look very happy," said Dad. The car stopped at the intersection. Jan gunned the engine, and the rear tire kicked up sand.

Who cared about Jan? Todd needed to know what Dad was thinking. Did he believe him? Did he think the guy in the first house acted strange?

They turned left at Twenty-first Street and headed for the car.

Dad started the engine and let it idle. "I think for the next few weeks, you and Kevin should forget about using the canoe."

Now he knew. "You don't believe us." It was more of a statement than a question.

His father turned toward him. "I'm not sure what to believe. You told me there would be a mark from the canoe and two sets of footprints. They weren't there. You told me you saw a burglary, yet the police and everyone on Huron Street say no burglary took place."

Todd pressed his feet into the floorboard. "Maybe the guy in that white house is lying," he said.

"Why would he lie?" asked Dad. "It doesn't make sense."

"It would if they were hiding something," said Todd. "Maybe that's why they're so unfriendly."

"There are a lot of people who don't speak to their neighbors," countered Dad. "We don't know the names of the people who live on the other side of Mr. Pritchard."

Todd couldn't think of a comeback. There wasn't anything left that would prove they were telling the truth.

"Until I find out what really happened, the canoe is off limits." Dad turned back to the steering wheel and put the car into gear.

As the car accelerated, so did Todd's anger. He folded his arms across his chest and stared out the window. It's not fair, he thought. Someone was lying, and he was paying the price. He took a deep breath. He would find out what was going on, no matter how long it took. But where could he start?

La

ble pho ... was the one good thing Jan had brought to the house. He punched in Kevin's number.

"Hello?" answered Mrs. Jarvis.

"Is Kevin there?" asked Todd.

"Just a minute," she replied.

"Hi," said Kevin, picking up the extension.

Todd waited for Mrs. Jarvis to hang up. "Can you get out of the house?"

"Sure, what's up?" asked Kevin.

"I want to bike over to Juniper and check some things out."

if those two

confidently. "Why
to a place they've al-

you're right. I'll meet you by
fifteen minutes."
witched off the phone. The plan was
m to go incognito so he changed into a
ir of jeans and a sweatshirt. He grabbed his sunglasses and Minnesota Timberwolves cap. Usually he avoided wearing any kind of cap. Whenever he took one off, the cowlick by his part stood straight up, and he hated that. He thought it made him look like a little kid. But today it was necessary. Carefully he pulled the bill down until it touched the top of the frames. He looked in the mirror. Confident that no one from this morning would recognize him, he pulled out his shoebox of important junk. Beneath an old shoelace and minature foam basketball, just to the right of his compass, lay his old watch.

Todd bounded down the steps, returned the

phone to the table, then peeked into the living room. Dad was sitting on the couch watching a basketball game on television.

"I'm going for a bike ride."

"Okay," said Dad. "Be home by six for dinner."

Before his father had finished the word "dinner," Todd had opened the door leading to the garage. Below the canoe, his BMX bike leaned against the wall. In the daylight, the deep gouges and jagged vertical line looked even worse. Maybe if he pedaled as fast as possible, he could forget about the damage to the canoe.

When he reached the bike path along Lakewood Drive, he tried to keep up with the fifteen- and eighteen-speeds. Bike after bike whizzed by, the riders hunched over, concentrating on the path in front of them. His legs tired and he slowed down. Overall, Todd was satisfied with his bike. You couldn't do a decent wheelie on a speed bike, nor could you jump things like he could with his BMX. It responded to his slightest touch, just like the canoe.

When he reached the bridge over the channel, he pulled up next to the concrete retaining wall and looked out at Sanctuary Island. Several white egrets sat in the treetops.

"Hi," said Kevin, pulling up to him.

"Remember when we came back last night, and the geese were making all that racket?"

"Yeah," said Kevin. "I've never heard them make that much noise before."

"I wonder what was scaring them." Todd looked back at the island.

"Maybe someone's dog swam out there," suggested Kevin.

"Why would a dog swim way out there?" asked Todd. "If he was hungry, all he'd have to do is tip over someone's garbage can."

"I know!" said Kevin, his eyes growing wide. "A giant fifteen-foot muskie weighing one hundred and fifty pounds jumped out of the water. The huge mouth with its razor-sharp teeth began munching down geese."

"Very funny," said Todd, shaking his head. Leave it to his friend to try and make him laugh when he was being too serious. Usually he appreciated Kevin's humor, but not today. Something about the geese last night bothered him.

It was like taking a multiple-choice quiz and not studying for it. He knew parts of the answer, but not enough to tell if it was *a, b,* or *c*.

"Come on, let's go," said Kevin. "I have to be home by five-thirty."

They crossed Lakewood Drive and took a right on Travers Road.

"Did your parents believe you?" asked Todd, as Kevin rode alongside.

"Last night they did," answered Kevin. "Boy, you should've seen the look on Sam's face when I told him what happened. He forgot all about that junker car and girls and asked me everything."

"Do they still believe you?" asked Todd.

Kevin sucked in his lower lip. "I'm not sure."

Bikes were coming from the opposite direction, and Kevin slowed down to fall behind. As soon as they passed, he pulled even again.

"Your dad called my dad this morning and told him what the police said. After that he asked me if we were telling the truth."

"Same here," said Todd. "I even convinced my father to go over to Huron Street with me.

There was somebody home at every house and they *all* denied being robbed."

"Someone's lying," said Kevin, then he pulled ahead.

Todd knew that when Kevin was confused or upset, he pedaled faster. Now that Kevin had that used mountain bike, Todd had to struggle to keep up. It used to be the other way around; Kevin huffing and puffing on his old BMX while Todd, up ahead, teased him into catching up.

Kevin had told him his parents had gotten him the mountain bike so he'd exercise more and lose some weight. And if Todd ever breathed a word of that to any of the guys, especially Jackson or Terry, Kevin threatened to pin him to the ground and pour a dozen leeches down his throat.

"Turn left at Twenty-first Street," yelled Todd, racing to catch up.

"Now where?" asked Kevin. He stopped and waited for Todd.

"We'll take a right up there on Huron Street. I want to ride down to the end of the block, turn around, then come back again."

Kevin nodded. They rode to the intersection

and turned right. After bouncing over the rough railroad tracks, they passed another hundred feet of trees. Finally the houses came into view. The street sloped toward Polaski's, and they coasted down the west side.

Todd hadn't noticed it earlier, but on the north end of Baldy's house there was another thick stand of timber. What a perfect place for a burglary, thought Todd. As long as the two guys entered from the back, no one would notice. He circled a couple of times, then steered the bike back the way they came.

They were passing the two-story house when the garage door opened. Todd glanced over his shoulder and saw Baldy and a much younger woman, with big gold earrings, walk into the garage.

Todd put his bike into high gear and raced past the trees toward the railroad tracks. Just before the tracks he veered to the left. "Hurry!" he called to Kevin. He jumped off the bicycle and shoved it into the brush.

Kevin stumbled off his bike and knelt down next to him. "Did you see something?" A few seconds later the car appeared.

"When my dad and I came over earlier, the guy in that white Audi acted real funny when we mentioned a burglary. He also said his wife didn't feel well."

"Maybe that was his daughter," said Kevin.

"Daughters don't play with the back of their dads' necks. She was doing the same thing Jan does to my dad."

"But that still doesn't mean he's the one that's lying," said Kevin.

"There's more," said Todd. "The guy who lives at the end of the street says nobody knows who these people are and that they're real unfriendly."

"I don't know. . . ." said Kevin, shaking his head.

Todd decided to try a different approach. "How long was it from the time the guys disappeared into the tunnel until we saw them again?"

Kevin thought a moment. "Fifteen minutes maybe, twenty tops."

"Right," said Todd. "That's not a lot of time. From where they landed in the canoe, it's a straight shot to that guy's patio doors." An idea popped into his head. "And since they're not home, it's a perfect time to take a look around."

"What if one of the neighbors catches us?" asked Kevin.

"Don't worry," said Todd. "There are lots of trees around Baldy's house. No one will see us. Come on."

They dragged their bikes farther into the brush and covered them with dead branches. Todd looked around to get his bearings. They weren't as far down as Dad and he had been earlier. If they angled toward the lake just a little, they should come out somewhere between the garage and the path. After fifty feet, the white siding became visible. Ten feet from the edge of the lawn, he squatted down. They were halfway between the house and the path.

"See anybody else around?" asked Todd, scanning the windows for any sign of movement. Behind him, he heard the familiar crunch of a fingernail being chewed.

"No," answered Kevin. He removed his little finger from his mouth.

"Let's go." Todd jumped up and dashed across the lawn. When he reached the back wall of the garage, his heart was racing. He didn't know if it was from excitement or exertion.

Slowly he raised his head and peeked into the garage. Except for a two-wheeled trash can near the door, it was bare. It didn't even look like a garage. No ladders or lawn mower, none of the junk people usually stash in a garage. On the right wall, a door led into the house.

Suddenly he realized Kevin hadn't followed him. Turning around he motioned for his friend to join him. Kevin stepped out of his hiding place and lumbered across the grass.

"Chicken," said Todd, when Kevin joined him.

"No sense in the both of us getting caught," he whispered.

"Uh-huh." Todd didn't believe that line for a minute.

"Really!" said Kevin. "Who'd go get help if this guy caught you?"

Todd tossed him a disgusted look, then continued onto the cement-slab patio. The drapes on the sliding glass doors were drawn, so he couldn't see inside. He pulled on the handle.

"Todd!" squeaked Kevin.

"Relax," said Todd. "It's locked." He heard a sigh of relief.

Crouching down, he turned the corner where the main part of the house jutted outward. He crept along the wall until he reached the first set of windows. Cautiously he inched his head upward. His eyes darted around the room. In front of him was a breakfast area with a small table and four chairs. The kitchen stretched out beyond that and on the other side of it, there was a formal dining room. The patio doors were to the left and sitting on the floor next to the glass were a pair of muddy shoes and a brown plastic pail.

In Todd's mind, a puzzle piece fell into place. Baldy must've made that water-soaked set of footprints down by the lake. He probably used the bucket to wash away the mark from the canoe and the other two sets of footprints. All right, one mystery solved. But why would he go to so much trouble? Unless . . .

Todd bent down again and scurried toward the large picture window. Slowly he raised his head. A flash of movement on his left startled him. He dropped to the ground, listening for any sound that meant they had been caught, but all he could hear was the rapid thudding of his own heartbeat.

Kevin chuckled softly. "Who's a chicken now?"

Todd jumped to his feet and looked in the window. A huge gray cat sat perched on the back of a stuffed chair. Its pink mouth opened and closed everytime it meowed. Todd laughed. He had been more scared than he'd thought.

Together the two of them looked around the room. The left wall had an opening leading into the breakfast area. Across the room, there was a huge red brick fireplace. Suddenly Todd felt Kevin's cold and clammy hand on his arm. He followed Kevin's gaze to the right. An entertainment center covered most of the wall. Three slots were open, one above the television and two between the speakers. Black wires hung limp, waiting to be attached somewhere.

"You were right about this guy," said Kevin.

Todd nodded his head slowly. "But how are we going to prove it?"

Chapter Six

After waving good-bye to Kevin at the bridge, Todd headed home. When he turned the corner of Windom Avenue, he saw Jan. Her shoulder-length auburn hair was tied back into a ponytail, and she was shooting baskets. At first he was surprised—he'd never seen her do that before, then he thought about this morning and how Dad believed her before him. His anger returned.

"Hi," she said, as he zoomed by her.

Todd ignored her. Inside the garage, he slammed on his brakes. The rear tire left a skid mark two feet in length. The door leading to the backyard was open and he could smell lighter fluid.

"Have a good ride?" asked Dad, standing back from the flaming grill.

"Yeah," answered Todd. He plopped down in a lawn chair. "What are we having for dinner?"

"You and I are having hamburgers—Jan's having chicken."

Figured. At least she was consistent. He hadn't once seen her eat red meat. The sound of the basketball being dribbled, then bouncing off the backboard tugged at his curiosity. "I didn't know she played."

"Played in college," said Dad.

The sounds stopped, and Jan appeared in the doorway. "How about a little two on one?"

Dad looked at him. Todd shook his head no. Jan shrugged her shoulders and disappeared back into the garage.

"Come on," coaxed Dad. "Help me out. Last time I played against her, she beat me by twenty-six points."

"Okay," Todd relented. The two of them walked out onto the driveway.

"We can only play twenty minutes," said Dad. "Then I have to put the meat on."

She let them have the ball first. From the edge of the driveway, Todd threw the basketball to his dad, but Jan got a hand on it. Two strides later, she made a lay-up.

"Two points," said Jan, smiling.

"See what I mean," said Dad.

Again Todd tossed the ball into play. Dad faked right, went left and caught the ball. He took a jump shot, but it bounced off the rim. Jan grabbed the rebound. She went up for a shot—two more points. This time when Todd threw the ball to his father, it was bounced back to him. He took a shot and it swished through the hoop.

"All right!" cried Dad. "At least we won't get skunked."

Dad tossed the ball to Todd. Jan managed to steal it, but missed her shot. Back and forth they went. Jan made most of her shots, and the two of them made half of theirs.

"That's it," declared Dad, bending over, his hands on his knees. "Time to put the meat on."

Todd could see the sweat running down his cheek.

"I had twenty-eight," said Jan. "What about you guys?"

His father looked at him.

"I think we had eighteen," answered Todd.

"Sounds good to me," said Dad. He wiped his face with his T-shirt.

Todd bounced the basketball while the two of them disappeared into the house. He pretended to fake to the right and at the same time bounce the ball backward through his legs. Trying to pivot back to the left, he almost tripped. Jan had used that move a couple of times. In fact, she had used several moves he would like to see again. His father returned with the meat, and Todd followed him onto the patio.

Dad laid the meat on the grill. "I called about the canoe this afternoon."

Todd swallowed. "What did they say?"

"The salesman we talked to last fall told me that they have a repair kit we can buy. If that doesn't work, then we'll have to take it to an automobile body shop that does fiberglass repairs."

Todd slumped in his chair. Body shops were expensive. Someone had dented the fender on his mom's car, and she had paid four hundred dollars to have it fixed. All of a sudden Todd had this urge to put the two burglars on the grill and let them cook until they came up with the money.

"I have fifty dollars in the bank," said Todd.

"I don't think we'll have to touch your money," said Dad. "Hopefully, I'll be able to fix the canoe."

Jan came out carrying a tray with buns, plates, a container of potato salad, and three large glasses of lemonade. She set the tray on the picnic table. Todd reached for a glass and downed half of its contents.

"There's more in the refrigerator," said Jan, as she stretched out in the lounger.

"Well, did you get your frustrations worked out?" asked Dad.

"Certainly did," said Jan. She lifted her glass toward both of them. "Thanks to you guys."

Todd didn't understand what was going on. Why was she toasting them?

Dad must've spotted the look of confusion on

his face. "Jan's buyers overheard our conversation with the Polaskis and used the robbery as an excuse not to buy the house.

So that's why Jan had looked so angry when she drove by them.

"At first I was angry with you two, but then I realized these buyers had given me excuses on four previous houses. My intuition tells me they're really not serious about buying."

Dad shook his head. "You and your intuition."

"Don't laugh," she said. "If it hadn't been for my intuition, we wouldn't have gotten married."

"What?" Todd watched his father stand there holding the spatula.

"As soon as I saw that high school picture of you with that basketball between your knees, my intuition said we should get serious."

Todd remembered the picture. It sat on the bookcase at his grandmother's house. Sitting beside it was his baby picture and—suddenly a thought occurred to him. Pictures! Of course! That's how he'd prove the guy on Huron Street was lying. He was so excited about his idea that at first he didn't hear his father.

"Your hamburger's ready," he repeated.

Todd wolfed down his dinner, then excused himself. Hurrying to his room, he tried to remember where the camera was. In the second dresser drawer, he looked under a pile of shirts; there was his camera, but he needed film. The drugstore was the closest, and it was open until nine. He took the steps two at a time and when he reached the bottom, he peeked out the window. Dad and Jan were still sitting on the patio. Picking up the telephone, he punched in Kevin's number.

"Hello?" answered Kevin.

"I figured out how to solve our problem."

"How?" asked his buddy.

"We'll take pictures."

There was silence on the other end. Finally Kevin protested, "But we can't just break in."

"We don't have to," said Todd. "We'll put the camera up to the window and take pictures that way."

"Will they turn out?" Kevin sounded doubtful.

"I've taken pictures through car windows and they've turned out. Why wouldn't it work through a picture window?"

Again there was a pause. "What if the people are home?"

"We'll just have to wait until they leave," answered Todd. "Let's go over tomorrow."

"I can't," said Kevin. "We're going to church in the morning, then we're leaving to visit my aunt. She lives way out in the boonies. We won't be back until late tomorrow night."

Todd was disappointed. "I guess I'll have to go by myself."

"Geez," said Kevin. "I wish I could get out of going."

"I'll tell you how it went on Monday."

"First thing Monday," said Kevin, then he hung up.

Todd clicked off and laid the phone back on the table. He didn't like the idea of going over by himself, but he knew it had to be done, and the sooner the better.

* * *

Sunday morning when he awoke, the sun was shining. Todd was glad. The sunshine would make the pictures turn out better. Just in case Dad was still asleep, he pulled his door open quietly. He was tiptoeing down the steps when he heard voices, then his name.

"I've been thinking about what happened to Todd and Kevin," said Jan. He froze on the steps and strained to hear. "When they came home," she continued, "Todd was wearing Kevin's sweatshirt."

"How come you remember that?" asked Dad.

"Because it was too big for him," answered Jan, "and when they came out of the bathroom, Kevin had his sweatshirt on and the blanket wrapped around his waist."

"What are you getting at?" asked his father.

Todd grasped the railing and leaned forward. Now it would come out. Somehow Jan would sway his dad's opinion against him, but this time he would catch her and be able to defend himself. Putting one foot on the next step, he readied himself.

"If they had swamped the canoe," said Jan, "wouldn't Kevin's sweatshirt have been wet, too?"

His dad was silent.

Hey! She was right! Todd almost fell when he let go of the railing.

"Yes," answered his father. "Unless Kevin was on shore or somehow managed to jump out near shore." He paused. "That still doesn't explain why a burglary wasn't reported."

Todd wanted to bolt down the stairs and explain to him that the guy on Huron Street was lying, but then it would still be his word against Baldy's and nothing would be solved. It was better to wait until he had the pictures; then he'd have proof.

"You know I have to be real careful in this situation," said his dad. "I have to be firm so he doesn't think he can push his limits just because you're here. So until this thing is cleared up, I have to stick to my decision about the canoe."

Todd crept back to his room and sat on the bed. It sounded like Jan believed them. He wasn't sure how he felt about that. It was good to know someone believed him, but Jan? He opened the door again, this time letting it bang against the rubber stopper. When he rounded the corner of the dining room, they were both sitting at the table reading the Sunday paper.

"Hi," said Todd, heading for the refrigerator.

"Ready for the big game today?" asked Dad. He held up the sports page. Twins Try to Sweep was the headline.

Todd stopped. He'd forgotten all about the baseball game. Dad always went to at least one of the games when the Yankees were in town.

"You two have fun," said Jan. "I have an open house at one o'clock." She rose from the table and disappeared into the bathroom.

"I thought we'd leave about eleven-fifteen," said Dad. "We have to stop and get gas, then drive over and pick up Roger." Roger was Dad's friend from work.

Todd looked at the clock. It was almost ten. "Shoot," he muttered. There wasn't enough time to go over to Huron Street. Once he got there, he'd just have to turn around and come back.

He shook his head. It would have to be an exciting ball game to take his mind off his plans for later.

The game went into extra innings and they didn't make it home until after five o'clock. Todd hurried to his room and put the camera in his left shirt pocket and his sunglasses in the right. He pulled his new Twins cap farther down on his forehead, then went downstairs to grab his bike.

On the way over to Balsam Lake, Kevin's question kept snaking its way into his mind. What if the people were home? He'd just have to wait until they left, he decided. What if they didn't leave? Dad would expect him to be home by dark. If he couldn't get the pictures tonight, he would come back tomorrow evening, and if that didn't work out, he'd have to think of something else.

When he reached Huron Street, he stopped and put on the sunglasses. First he needed to check out the front of the house to see if the car was there. He didn't want Baldy recognizing him.

Slowly he coasted down the street. The roof of the Audi was visible through the garage door window. He made a wide sweeping turn and headed back the way he came. This time, he noticed, the dining room drapes were closed.

Once he reached the spot where they had pulled over earlier, he hid his bike in the bushes. He made his way toward the house, careful not to angle in as far as he had on Saturday. Fifteen feet from the edge of the lawn was an old stump surrounded by a tangle of brush—a perfect hiding place. He could see the road, the side and back walls of the garage, and the patio doors.

The drapes were open and he could see movement in the living room, but not enough to tell what was going on. It looked like he was going to be there awhile. He removed his cap and the sunglasses and settled down next to the stump.

A mosquito buzzed around his head. "Go away," he mumbled, swatting at it with his hand. Another mosquito hovered near his arm. He was thankful it was early in the season; otherwise there would be dozens swarming around him.

An hour went by, and his right leg had fallen asleep. It tingled as he massaged it. The woman he'd seen getting into the car yesterday came into the breakfast area. Her back to Todd, she stood in the archway leading to the living room. A few seconds later, she turned around and Baldy entered the room behind her. He was carrying some boxes. Todd squinted. He could make out the letters VCR printed on one of them. Quickly he scrambled to his knees. Had they bought replacements already? His stomach sank. Now how was he going to get pictures? Then he had an idea. Removing the camera from his pocket, he peered into the viewfinder and snapped the shutter. Would the picture turn out or was he too far away for the little camera to get a clear shot?

Baldy was still holding the boxes when he began gesturing at the patio doors and at the woman. He looked angry. The woman lowered her head and nodded. After a few more gestures, he stopped. The woman walked over to him, and he turned his face toward the sliding glass door. She kissed him on the cheek.

Todd ducked behind the stump and held his breath. He hoped he hadn't been spotted. The sound of the garage door opening scared him into action. Grabbing his cap, he rose to a crouched position and prepared to flee.

Baldy appeared on the driveway, pushing the two-wheeled garbage can. He set it down near the street, then went back to the house. The garage door closed. The lid of the garbage can was raised, and a cardboard flap hung out over the side.

Todd crept through the brush to get a better look. A picture showing the lettering on the boxes was the only option left. He could just get up and walk out there, but what if Baldy saw him? On foot, he might not be able to get away.

He took his bike out of its hiding place. Slowly he coasted up to the garbage can and when his body was even with it, he stopped.

The box with the flap hanging over the side had the letters *VCR* printed on it. The second box was upside down, but Todd could read the words *Stereo Receiver*. There was another smaller box underneath those two. Even though he couldn't see the printing, he was sure it had contained a CD player just a few minutes ago.

A picture postcard stuck out between the boxes. He grabbed it, hoping he could find out Baldy's name. Quickly he scanned the message. "Free vacation in Florida. Call this number today!" It was addressed to Lawrence Ollney in Winnepeg, Manitoba, Canada. Why was it here? wondered Todd.

Nervous now, Todd stuffed the card in his back pocket, then took a picture. He was just about to take another shot when the garage door opened. Baldy came out carrying a paper bag.

"Hey! What are you doing?" he yelled.

Todd snapped the shutter, then shoved the camera into his pocket. Grabbing the handlebars, he sped toward Travers Road. When he reached the bike path, he glanced over his shoulder; he didn't see anyone chasing him so he sat down and relaxed.

Near the south end of Balsam Lake Todd got the creepy feeling that he wasn't alone. He whipped his head to the left—no one on the path. He checked the other direction—someone was on the road! In the distance a white car, he couldn't tell what make, snaked its way along Travers Road. Afraid, he pedaled faster. There's more than one white car in Hidden Springs, he tried to tell himself. He looked back again. The car was gaining. It was the Audi.

Stay near people, he told himself. Behind him two men on racing bikes were flying toward him. Desperately he tried to stay ahead of them, but within seconds they had caught up, and as he opened his mouth to say something, they whizzed by him.

On the walking path two blocks ahead, a woman was out jogging. He veered across the grassy area separating the two paths and raced to catch up to her. When he was still a block away, the woman turned up the first driveway on Burnside Lane and disappeared into the house.

In seconds he would reach the railroad tracks that crossed Travers Road. There the bicycle and walking paths converged with the roadway. The Audi pulled even. Together they raced toward the tracks. Suddenly the car surged ahead. Oh God, thought Todd, he's going to catch me! The

Audi swerved left, blocking the oncoming lane and both paths. The white fender loomed thirty feet in front of him. Gripping the handlebars tightly, Todd slammed on his brakes. He prayed his rear tire wouldn't hit sand and slide out from under him.

He jumped off and began pushing the bike at a run. He darted through the weeds to reach the railroad tracks. Baldy jumped out of the car, but before he could chase Todd, a car coming from Alpine Lake screeched to a halt and honked. Todd slowed enough to watch Baldy hop back in the car, slam it into reverse, then peel out back the way he came.

Todd stumbled to a stop and tried to catch his breath. "Boy, did I luck out," he muttered. He wiped the sweat from his forehead. Up ahead the old wooden bridge crossed the tracks.

Todd sucked in his breath in disbelief. The Audi rolled onto the bridge and stopped. Slowly the front passenger window lowered. What if Baldy has a gun? Frantically, Todd looked around. There were no people nearby, and worse, he was out in the open. He crashed into the brushy embankment on his right, dragging the bike with him. He had to get near people!

Raspberry thorns and tree branches snagged his clothes and scratched his face and arms. A young sapling became entangled in his rear tire. "Come on!" pleaded Todd, as he yanked on the handlebars. Finally the stubborn tree broke. Another fifteen feet, then a grassy backyard appeared. Panting, he pushed the bike onto the lawn. He hit Farrell Street just as the car left the bridge. It was one block to Lakewood Drive, people, and safety.

The sound of the motor grew louder. Out of the corner of his eye, Todd could see the white fender inching closer to his rear tire. He's trying to hit me! His mind screamed. His eyes searched for an escape route. Halfway down the block was a driveway. He swerved to his left, his tires hugging the curb. Sixty feet to go. Behind him the engine revved. Thirty feet. The white menace closed in. The curb ended. Todd swerved onto the sidewalk.

Seconds later he burst into the intersection just as a car at the stop sign accelerated. The driver slammed on his brakes. The rear wheel of Todd's bike screeched as he made the sharp left around the car's bumper. He regained his balance in time to hear the angry driver shouting at him.

"Crazy kid! You wanna get killed?"

Todd snaked his way through the oncoming traffic. A second car's horn blasted away, so did a third, but Todd didn't care. Feeling safe now, he turned his head to look back. The Audi had to turn right. His pulse started to return to normal. That had been a close call—too close.

Chapter Seven

Sunday night Todd tossed and turned as the same dream played over and over in his mind. Each time, the white fender of the Audi came closer. Then, as if he were watching from a distance, the bumper struck his rear tire and he saw his body flying through the air.

A cannon blast of thunder went off above the house, and he bolted upright. For a moment, he was unsure of his surroundings. Suddenly lightning illuminated his dresser, and his breathing slowed.

He got up and peered out the window. Under the streetlight, he could see the strong wind and driving rain pounding the trees. Shivering, he crawled back into bed and turned on the light. Lying on the floor was a *Sports Illustrated* magazine. Todd picked it up and tried to concentrate on the article about which teams were expected to make the NBA finals. Forty minutes later he still wasn't sleepy. Finally, after the sixth article, his eyelids closed.

The morning sun was shining when he rolled over and turned the alarm off. Burying his head under the pillow, he wished he could sleep another eight hours. But that was impossible. He had to meet Kevin at school, tell him what had happened, and get the film developed.

Downstairs, Jan stood next to the stove. "I'm having pancakes—" She stared at him. "What happened to you?"

At first Todd didn't know what she meant. Then he realized she must be looking at his scratches. The one on his forehead wasn't bad, but there were several longer and deeper ones on his forearms. "I rode into a bush."

"That'll do it," she said.

Last night when he came home, Dad and Jan were still sitting outside. He had gone straight to his room and not come out the rest of the evening.

She lifted a couple of pancakes. "Want some?"

"Sure," answered Todd. The first time she had made pancakes he'd been hesitant to try them, fearing they would be full of all kinds of healthy, nutty things, but they weren't. They were just plain old pancakes, and just plain good.

The streets were still wet from the storm, and he steered the bike away from the larger puddles. It wasn't until he'd gone a couple of blocks that he realized he was looking for the white Audi. Don't worry, he told himself, Baldy doesn't know where you live. How could he? Suddenly Todd remembered his father introducing the two of them after Baldy had opened the door. The blood drained from his face. There are lots of John Bensons in the phone book, he tried to reassure himself. It was a common name for this area. He chewed the inside of his lip. But how many live in Hidden Springs? At that moment Todd wished he could change his name.

When he reached school, he looked around one last time, then locked his bike to the rack.

In front of his open locker, he reached into his backpack.

A hand clamped down on his shoulder. "Tell me," said Kevin.

Todd jumped and dropped everything.

"Sorry," apologized Kevin. "Didn't mean to scare you."

"I know," said Todd, picking up his backpack. "I guess I'm just a little jumpy today."

His friend studied him. "You look like you had a fight with a cat. What happened?"

"Baldy—"

Kevin interrupted, "Who's Baldy?"

"That's what I call the guy in the white Audi," said Todd. Kevin nodded. "He chased me last night in his car. I had to use the railroad tracks on the south end of Balsam to make my get away. Even then he almost caught me on Farrell Street."

Kevin's eyes widened. "This sounds better than television."

"Almost got me, too, but I swerved up a driveway and made it to Lakewood Drive. Then I biked against the traffic to get away."

"Wow!" said his friend. "But why did he chase you?"

"He caught me taking pictures of his garbage can and the boxes from his replacement VCR and stereo receiver." He pulled out the roll of film and waved it in front of Kevin.

"Geez," said Kevin. "I wish I could have gone with you."

Todd watched him lean against the next locker. Just as well he hadn't, thought Todd. He probably wouldn't have gotten away. "I found this, too," he said, pulling the postcard from his pack.

"What is it?" asked Kevin.

"I'm not sure," answered Todd. "It might not be anything, but don't you think it's strange that Baldy would have a postcard addressed to someone in Winnepeg, Canada?"

"Yeah," agreed Kevin. "We sometimes get mail that's supposed to have been delivered next door, sometimes even the next block, but the next country?"

"I thought we could call the number on the back and see what happens."

"Good idea," said Kevin, handing him the card. The bell rang and they ran for class.

Through science, gym, and history, Todd barely paid attention. His mind kept wandering back to the events of the past three days. Friday night and getting chased, Saturday and everybody denying the burglary, then last night and getting chased again. What was he getting himself into?

In English class, he pulled the postcard out of his pocket and placed it on the desk. There were three separate photographs on the front. The first one showed a couple, wearing swimsuits, walking hand in hand along a deserted beach. The second shot was an aerial view of people lying on a beach and palm trees in the background. The third photograph had a hotel in the background and an empty beach in front of it. Across the top *Congratulations* was printed in orange.

On the back there was a telephone number, same area code as his own. It said to call within five days to claim a prize of three nights and four days free in a hotel in one of Florida's finest cities—Tampa, Orlando, or Miami.

Suddenly Todd noticed the snickers of his classmates. Mr. Rand, his English teacher, was striding toward him. Todd tried to slide the postcard under a notebook.

"I'll take that," said Mr. Rand. "Perhaps now we'll be able to ensure your complete attention." Todd could feel his face burning. "See me after class."

Thankfully everyone's attention shifted away from him as Mr. Rand started writing a list of humorous dangling participles on the blackboard. For the rest of the period, Todd paid attention. When the bell rang, he waited for everyone to leave before going to Mr. Rand's desk.

"Well," said his teacher, "this is hardly what I expected to find."

Usually Mr. Rand intercepted notes being passed to another student. Once he'd even confiscated a packet of drugs. The teacher stroked his graying beard. Todd was positive he did this to make his students feel uncomfortable. After a few seconds had passed, he had to admit it worked.

"Your attention has been wandering lately,"

he said finally. "Today it was especially apparent you were not with us."

Todd was silent.

"You've got an *A* going in this class, and I'd hate to see you lose it this late in the year." Todd nodded. "So," he said, handing him the card, "are your parents thinking about using this vacation offer?"

Todd took the card. "No." He was surprised by the question.

"I'm glad to hear that," said Mr. Rand. "Most of these offers for vacations are scams, rip-offs." He shook his head. "My wife and I found out the hard way. We paid our membership fee and what did we get? Nothing, absolutely nothing. Of course we only lost a couple of hundred dollars. Many people lose much more."

"But the card says the vacation is free," said Todd.

"You're led to *believe* the vacation is free," corrected Mr. Rand, "because of the 'Congratulations' printed on the front and the bold lettering on the back. But it's really just a ruse, designed to get you to call the phone number.

If you read carefully, you'll see it says 'vacation *offer*.' That's the key."

Todd found the words *fantastic vacation offer* in small print on the fourth line. He looked up to see Mr. Rand studying him.

"Would you like to learn more about this kind of scam operation?"

"You bet," said Todd eagerly.

"Go to the school library and look in the most recent *Reader's Guide to Periodical Literature*." Todd scribbled the name down on the back of his notebook. "Look under the heading 'Tourist Trade.' There should be several articles detailing this type of fraud."

"Thanks," said Todd, jotting down tourist trade. He left Mr. Rand and rushed to the lunchroom.

"Hurry up and eat," he said, setting a tray down next to Kevin.

"How come?" mumbled Kevin, his mouth full.

"We're going to the library."

Kevin choked on his pizza. "On lunch hour, are you kidding?"

Todd slapped the card on the table. "If Baldy

is the one sending these postcards to people, it means he might be running a scam. We can find out more information in the library."

Kevin swallowed. "Hey, that might explain why he wouldn't report a burglary."

"Exactly," said Todd, and he wolfed down his pizza slice.

"Where's the *Reader's Guide to Periodical Literature?*" asked Todd, when they entered the library.

"Against the far wall, second desk," answered the student librarian.

Todd looked at the clock. They had fifteen minutes before the bell rang. He pulled down the newest *Reader's Guide to Periodical Literature*. Quickly he flipped through the pages until he reached the *T*s.

"Here it is," he said. Kevin looked over his shoulder. Todd ran his forefinger down the list of magazine articles. "Travel Scams: A Costly Trip," was in *Newsweek*. He jotted down the month, date, and page number. A second article "Anatomy of a Travel Scam" was in *Read-*

er's Digest. Again he copied down the issue date and page number.

"Where do we find the magazines?" asked Kevin, looking around.

"Over here," said Todd, going to the wall unit containing white plastic holders.

"I found *Newsweek,*" said Kevin.

"Look for the January twenty-seventh issue, page forty-eight." Todd located the November copy of *Reader's Digest* and opened it to page eighty-six. The article was only two pages in length, and he finished before Kevin. He glanced at the clock. Five minutes remained before the bell rang. "Come on, read faster," he muttered softly.

"Talk about a rip-off!" he said, when Kevin finally looked up. "Promise people a vacation, take their money, then move on and change your name if too many people start complaining. Pretty slick."

"I'll say," agreed Kevin, as they switched magazines. "Even the ones that do get something end up paying more than if they had gone through a travel agency."

Todd wasn't finished with the *Newsweek* article when the bell rang. "Meet me by the bike rack after school. We'll go over to the mall and get the pictures developed at the one-hour photo store." Kevin gave him a thumbs-up sign, then left. Seven minutes later Todd shoved the magazine back into its holder and sprinted down the empty hall to his math class.

"So nice of you to take time out of your busy schedule to join us," said his teacher, Mrs. Carlisle.

His classmates, including his friend Jackson, laughed as he hurried to his desk. He wondered if Mrs. Carlisle would like a present. A small box with a bow on top and a garter snake inside. He shook his head. The way his luck was running lately, she'd probably like the snake and turn it into a pet.

Todd's mind wandered back to the pictures. They should prove he was telling the truth. Or would they? He chewed the inside of his lower lip. Baldy could always say he bought the VCR and stereo receiver for upstairs. Without a search warrant, they couldn't prove otherwise.

Even if Baldy *was* running a scam operation,

it would be difficult to uncover. The magazine articles had stated that since these operations used their high-pressure sales tactics over the phone, there was no paper trail. Geez! He rubbed his forehead. There had to be some way to stop Baldy from blocking all their shots.

Finally, at three o'clock, the last bell rang. Todd raced for his locker, dumped his books inside, then grabbed his backpack.

"Hey, Todd," called Jackson. "How about shooting some baskets today?"

"Can't," called Todd, "maybe later this week." He slammed the locker door shut.

Kevin was waiting for him by the bike rack. They took off for the mall. Twenty minutes later, they locked their bicycles to a No Parking sign.

"Have you got any money?" asked Todd, as they headed toward the photo store.

Kevin pulled out a worn billfold. "Two bucks and"—he counted his change—"fifty-three cents."

"I've got three-fifty," said Todd. "Hope that's enough." They walked up to the counter.

"May I help you?" asked the woman behind

the counter. She peered at them over squared-off glasses.

"I want to get these developed right away."

She took the film. "Name?"

"Todd Benson," he answered. "Can you tell me how much it will cost?"

"One-hour service on a twelve is seven-fifty."

"Seven-fifty!" said Todd. The woman raised an eyebrow. "But there's only three pictures on there that need developing."

"I'm sorry," she said. "We have to charge for the entire roll."

"Make it overnight," suggested Kevin.

"How much then?" asked Todd.

"Four-fifty," she answered.

"Okay," agreed Todd, reluctantly. "Overnight then."

"Are you sure?" she asked, raising an eyebrow again.

"Yes," snapped Todd, and he turned to walk away.

"Wait," she called. "I need your address and you need a claim ticket." She held the slip out to him and he told her his address. They left the store and stood in the middle of the mall.

"Now what?" asked Kevin, looking longingly at the candy store across from them.

Todd inhaled the sweet-smelling air. The store sold the best caramel corn in the city. Can't buy anything today, he thought wistfully. He needed his money for the film. "Let's go to my house and call the number on the card."

Two girls about their age sauntered by. One of them whispered to the other, then they snickered.

Kevin's face turned red. "Come on, let's get out of here." He stomped off toward the doors.

Todd hadn't heard what the first girl had whispered, but he overheard the second one. "Look how he bounces when he walks." Then they laughed again.

He ran after Kevin.

Chapter Eight

On the way back, Todd had to hustle to keep up with Kevin. He was glad when his friend took the shortcut to Alpine Lake and the bike path. When they reached the bridge over the channel, Todd slammed on his brakes.

"Did you see that?"

"See what?" asked Kevin.

Todd quickly turned the bike around and guided it back a few feet. Now where was it? He hopped off, letting the handlebars rest against the concrete retaining wall. It still wasn't visible. He moved two more steps to his right.

"What's wrong?" asked Kevin.

"Look," said Todd pointing.

Kevin got off his bike. "I don't see anything."

"Take one more step this way." He pulled on Kevin's shirtsleeve.

"Now I see it," he said. "Probably a pop can or a piece of foil. The wind last night could have blown anything onto the island."

Todd shook his head. "It looks too big for that."

Just then the bow of an aluminum canoe appeared from under the bridge. Todd watched it glide into view. A woman was seated in the bow, a black Labrador sat behind the center thwart, and a man relaxed in the stern, the paddle resting on his knees. Movement in the bushes alerted the dog, and he jumped up suddenly. His tail knocked the paddle off the man's knees so that it banged against the canoe. The hollow sound echoed over the water.

Something clicked in Todd's mind. Friday night and the geese honking, then that faraway sound. He looked at the shiny object again. What was it Jan had told him? He racked his brain trying to remember. Something about the police and their spotlight. That was it! On the way over to his house they had flashed their spotlight on Alpine Lake.

"The stuff's on the island!" blurted Todd.

"What stuff?"

"The stuff the two men stole. It's on the island."

"You're crazy," said Kevin. "Burglars sell their stolen goods for drugs or money. They don't leave it rot on some island." He shook his head.

"But what if they didn't have a choice?" asked Todd excitedly.

"What do you mean?"

"I think the geese were honking Friday night because the two men were on the island. That sound we heard was one of their paddles hitting the canoe as they were leaving."

Kevin narrowed his eyes. "But why would they stop on the island? It doesn't make sense."

"It would if they thought we had reached a phone and called the cops," said Todd. He was keyed up. Things were falling into place.

"Why would they think that?" asked Kevin.

"Because Jan told me that on the way over to our house the police flashed their spotlight on the lake. They were looking for us. The two burglars would've thought the police were looking for them. So instead of getting caught with the stuff, they dumped it on the island."

When Kevin didn't say anything right away, Todd knew he was partially convinced.

"It's possible, I suppose," he said finally.

Todd looked at the island. The reflection had grown faint. "If only we could get out there and find out for sure."

"How?" asked Kevin. "We can't use your canoe."

Todd thought for a minute. "Do you and Sam still have that two-man raft?"

"Sure," answered Kevin. "But it's been folded up for the last year and a half. I don't even know if it will float anymore."

"Come on," said Todd, looking at his watch. "We can plan more at my place. I want to call that number on the postcard before Jan gets home."

It was twenty minutes to five when they entered the kitchen. Todd pulled the postcard from his pocket. Slowly he pushed the numbers.

"Good afternoon, Dreams Are Yours Vacations. May I help you?"

Todd put his hand over the mouthpiece. "It's him" he whispered.

"Who?" asked Kevin.

"Baldy."

"Hello? Hello?" Baldy repeated.

Todd cleared his throat. "Yes," he tried to deepen his voice so that he'd sound older. "I received a postcard about a free vacation."

"What we have to offer," said Baldy, "is a wonderful, fun-filled three-night, four-day vacation in one of Florida's most exciting locations—Tampa, Orlando, or Miami. All you have to do is pay the small membership fee of one hundred and eighty-nine dollars to receive this and other fabulous vacation offers. It's so easy, and I'm sure you'll agree this is an extraordinary bargain. Now if you'll give me your name and credit card number, we'll get you lined up for this fantastic offer."

Todd put his hand over the mouthpiece again. "He wants my name!"

"Give him a fake one," whispered Kevin.

"My name's Roger," said Todd, his voice slightly higher than before.

"Okay, Roger," said Baldy. "If you'll give me your last name and credit card number, we can get you signed up for this once-in-a-lifetime offer."

"A-h-h." Todd's brain raced. "John," he stumbled over the word. "My last name's Johnson." Kevin rolled his eyes.

Todd knew he was blowing it, but he couldn't help it. Baldy's high-pressure sales pitch was making him nervous. If only he could remember some of the questions the magazines had said to ask. Baldy didn't say anything for a few seconds. Uh-oh, we've lost him, thought Todd.

"Okay, Mr. Johnson, if you'll just give your credit card number."

Todd was relieved. They still had a chance to find out something. "I don't have one."

"Well, we'll certainly take a check. I can have a courier at your house within the hour to pick it up. All I need is your address."

Todd's mind went blank. He couldn't think of a fake address. "How can you offer these vacations so cheap?" he blurted. There, he finally remembered one of the questions.

"We deal in volume," answered Baldy. "With our discounts many people find these vacations an irresistible bargain. Now if you'll just give me your address."

The sweat ran down the sides of Todd's rib cage. Baldy had an answer for everything. "A-h-h . . ."

Kevin spread his arms and pretended to be an airplane.

"What airline would I be flying?" asked Todd, trying not to laugh as Kevin circled the table.

"We deal only with the major carriers," answered Baldy. "Your address, please?"

Bingo! That was one of the vague answers the magazines said to watch out for.

Now Kevin pretended to be carrying suitcases.

"What hotel would I be staying at?" Todd's voice was back to normal.

Again Baldy hesitated, but this time his reply made the hairs on Todd's neck stand up. "We both know you're not *old* enough to have a checking account!" The phone was slammed down.

Stunned, Todd listened to the dial tone for a few seconds before putting the phone on the table. "He guessed."

"Guessed what?" asked Kevin.

"That I was too young and . . ."

"What?" Kevin leaned on the table.

"I think he recognized my voice," said Todd. "He kept wanting my address so that he could send a courier over to pick up a check."

"That's how they avoid mail-fraud charges," said Kevin. "Remember?"

"Yeah, I guess you're right." Todd tried to shrug off the fear he felt.

"What else did he say?"

"At first he kept asking for a credit card number just like the magazine articles said, and he wouldn't give me the name of an airline or hotel."

The door opened, and Jan walked in carrying a grocery bag. "Hi, guys," she said, as she set the bag on the kitchen counter. Todd slipped the postcard back into his pocket.

"I should go home," said Kevin.

"I'll come over later, and we can talk about that project."

"What project?" asked Kevin. Todd looked at him hard.

"Oh, yeah," said Kevin, "that project." He hurried for the door. "Bye."

"Good-bye," called Jan. "Big project for school?" She began to empty the bag.

"Yes," lied Todd.

"What class is it for?"

"Um, history," he answered. "I better do some homework." He hustled up to his room, then plopped down on the bed to think.

The stolen goods on the island and Baldy running a scam. Were they connected? How could they be? It was probably just a coincidence. Could Kevin possibly be right about the shiny object being a pop can? If only he could be certain before they risked getting into more trouble. Jan had a pair of binoculars she used for bird-watching. Maybe she'd let him use them.

A few minutes later Jan called, "Dinner's ready."

The meal went by quickly, and Todd was grateful she didn't ask him any more questions about their project.

"Can I use your binoculars?" he asked, as Jan began clearing the table.

She hesitated a moment, then said, "Sure. I'll go get them." Within a few seconds she returned. Carefully she unwound the soft leather strap. "They were my father's, so please be careful with them." She handed them over.

"Thanks," said Todd. With the binoculars securely around his neck, he biked to the bridge.

When he reached the concrete wall, he searched for the reflection. At first he didn't see anything. He moved to his right. Where was it? He willed it to shine as bright as it had earlier. After another step to his right, he spotted something. The image had grown faint with the lowering of the sun. It was definitely not a pop can. There were three separate strips of metal. Turning the focus knob, he tried to get a better view, but it began to blur. Was it the silverware? The strong wind last night could've blown the wooden cover off.

He hurried to Kevin's house. Sam's car was

in the driveway. The old brown Ford had one white door, a cracked windshield, and warped rusted-out fenders. Sam stood in front of the car, peering into the engine compartment. His grease-covered hand waved a greeting as Todd rode by him.

Kevin stepped into the garage as Todd laid his bike down. They removed the raft from the shelf, then began wiping away the heavy layer of dust surrounding the air valves. Todd started blowing air into the yellow-and-blue inflatable.

"What are you going to do with the raft?" asked Sam. He dropped a wrench into the tool box.

"We're taking it out on Alpine," answered Kevin.

"What happened to that fancy canoe?"

"It has a hole," answered Todd. He was feeling light-headed so he stopped blowing for a minute. "Are you going to be around in the morning?"

"I'll be here until ten-fifteen," answered Sam, "then I have to go to work."

Last week Todd had thought it was dumb for the teachers to have their staff meetings on a

Tuesday. Why not a Monday? But now he was glad there wouldn't be school tomorrow.

"He switched shifts with the day dishwasher so that he could have Friday night off for his big date with Nadia," said Kevin, rolling his eyes.

Todd had an idea. "We'll wash and wax your car if you take us and the raft over to Alpine tomorrow morning and wait for us."

"What?" Kevin stopped blowing into the raft.

Sam narrowed his eyes and looked at them. "What time do you want to go?"

"Six-thirty," answered Todd.

"Six-thirty! I don't know," said Sam, scratching his newly sprouted whiskers. "I like to sleep in. How come so early?"

"We want to get on the island before too many people come around," replied Todd.

"But why go to the island?" asked Sam.

"I'm almost positive the two men who chased us Friday night stashed the stolen items out there." He picked up the binoculars. "I double-checked with these," he said to Kevin.

"All right," said Sam. "But if the stuff isn't out there, you clean the inside of the car, too."

"Deal," said Todd.

Sam closed the car's hood, then went inside the house.

"That stuff better be there," growled Kevin, "or you're cleaning the car by yourself."

"It will be," said Todd, and they finished blowing air into the raft.

Chapter Nine

Tuesday morning the dew on the grass glistened as the sun rose higher. The morning songs of cardinals and robins followed Todd to the Jarvis house.

Kevin met him at the door. "We have to be quiet, my dad's still asleep." They padded through the kitchen toward the hallway.

"How you two ever got Sam to agree to get up this early, I'll never understand," said Mrs. Jarvis, shaking her head.

If she only knew the deal he'd made, thought Todd. He followed his friend to Sam's bedroom door. Kevin knocked, but there was no answer.

He opened the door and they slipped inside. Sam lay face down; a pillow covered part of his head. A car door handle and new windshield wipers lay on the dresser next to the bed.

Kevin nudged his brother on the shoulder. "Wake up."

"M-m-m?" mumbled Sam, as he turned his head toward Kevin. He opened his eyes and looked at his brother. "Beat it."

"You promised to help us," said Todd. "We're going to clean your car for your date with Nadia. Remember?"

Sam raised up to eyeball Todd. Then he dropped his head back onto the pillow and let out a long sigh. "I remember," he said. Slowly he put his legs over the side of the bed. "That car better be spotless when you're done."

Todd smiled. He hoped the fenders didn't fall off when they washed it.

Sam put on a grease-stained shirt and jeans and followed them into the garage. Kevin opened the rear passenger door and they squeezed the raft and paddles into the backseat, then climbed in the front seat. Still half-asleep, Sam almost missed the turn to Alpine Lake.

Todd glanced at his watch as they traveled along Lakewood Drive; it was quarter to seven. He'd seen a couple of people on bicycles and a few cars. Overall it was quiet, and that was the way he wanted it.

"Pull in here," said Todd, pointing to a parking spot next to a big elm. From where he wanted to launch the raft, it was a straight shot to the island. He hoped the stolen goods would be nearby.

Sam stopped the car, and Todd and Kevin wrestled the raft from the backseat. Even before they shut the door, Sam lay down and closed his eyes. When they reached the water, Todd climbed in first. Kevin handed him the oars, and he inserted them into the blue plastic rings, then his friend pushed the raft farther into the lake and stumbled in.

Todd could feel the water's iciness through the plastic. At first he had goose bumps. Five minutes later he wiped the sweat from his forehead. He felt like it was taking forever to get anywhere.

"There go the geese," said Kevin.

Todd turned around in time to see two adult geese and seven or eight goslings slip into the water. During the day they would leave the island and forage the grassy areas around the lake. As the raft inched closer to the goose family, the adults grew alarmed and started honking. Quickly they steered the goslings away from the intruders. Farther down the shoreline another goose family scurried into the water.

Todd was glad they were almost at the island. The muscles in his arms felt as limp as spaghetti noodles. With Kevin in the stern, his weight forced the bow of the raft up and out of the lake. That meant half of the paddles' blade area never touched water.

A park maintenance vehicle caught Todd's attention. He watched the small cart roll its way over the walking path. It pulled up next to a garbage can and stopped. The driver jumped out, yanked off the lid, removed the plastic bag, then threw it into the back of the cart. After replacing the bag and lid, he continued down the path, coming closer to where they had launched the raft. Todd nervously looked around. Forty feet of water separated them from the island. He hoped they wouldn't be spotted. Again the man jumped out, removed the lid, and pulled out the plastic bag. Todd saw him hesitate as he looked in their direction, but a few seconds later he got back into the cart and drove off.

"What's the matter?" asked Kevin.

"For a minute I thought we were going to get caught," answered Todd.

"Why?" asked Kevin. He craned his head around to see.

"A park maintenance guy spotted us, but he kept going. I think we're okay."

"I wonder what they do to you if they catch you on the island?"

"I don't know," said Todd, and he hoped they wouldn't find out.

After a few more strokes, he felt the bow scrape bottom. They carried the raft into the brush and hid it.

"The stuff can't be too far back," said Todd, glancing at the bridge over the channel. He scanned the area around him. Was this the spot or was it over farther? It looked so different now that he was here. "We'll just have to search this entire section."

The soft green of newly sprouted growth was everywhere. Thirty feet in, Todd stopped. When he bent down and leaned to his left, he could just barely see the bridge.

"Let's stand five feet apart and walk back and forth until we find the stuff."

"If it's here," said Kevin, chewing on a fingernail.

On their second sweep, Todd stepped over the charred half of a tree split by lightning. Only the base of the trunk still connected the two halves. The way the two pieces had fallen reminded Todd of a gull's wings when it rides on a wind current.

After the next round, Todd started to worry. The longer they were on the island, the greater the chance they would be caught. "It has to be here," he said, quickening his pace. He stepped over a freshly broken branch. A sheet of white paper caught his eye. Just garbage? Then he noticed the perforated edges and the holes. Todd thought it strange to find a sheet of computer paper out here. He picked it up and carefully unfolded the soggy sections.

"What have you got?" asked Kevin, walking toward him.

"I'm not sure," answered Todd, "probably

nothing." Quickly he scanned the sheet, names on the left side, dollar amounts in the middle. He was about to drop it and not waste any more time when he spotted Dreams Are Yours Vacations in the upper left-hand corner. "Can't be!" He looked at it more closely. There it was in black and white, Dreams Are Yours Vacations, and printed next to it the time and date, May 3, 5:30 P.M. That was Friday—the day of the burglary.

Kevin leaned over him. "Isn't that the name of the place we called?"

"Yeah," answered Todd, completely stumped.

"What's it doing out here?"

"I don't know," said Todd. "Let's hurry up and find the stolen goods, maybe that'll give us a clue why this is out here."

"You on the island!"

Todd and Kevin jumped at the amplified sound.

"You have ten seconds to get off that island or be arrested. One, two, three . . ."

"But we haven't found the stuff," Todd pleaded with the unknown voice.

"Forget it," said Kevin, pulling at him. "Come

on, let's go!" Todd folded the paper and stuffed it into his shirt pocket.

"Seven, eight . . ."

They raced to the raft and yanked it out of its hiding spot. After dropping it in the water, they jumped in, and Kevin began rowing. Todd could see the squad car on shore and parked next to it the maintenance cart.

By the way Kevin rowed, Todd knew he was scared. Short, fast strokes slapped the water. His right arm was stronger, which sent the raft veering off to the left.

"Come over here, you two," the voice commanded.

Todd peered at the tall, blue-clad figure standing next to the police car. It couldn't be, he tried to tell himself. He glanced at his watch; it was seven-forty. When they reached the half-way point, the maintenance person climbed into his cart and drove away.

"I hope they don't take us down to juvenile hall," said Kevin. Beads of sweat ran down the sides of his cheeks.

A few minutes later they pulled up on shore. Todd looked up to see Officer Grady towering over them.

"Well, if it isn't our two friends from Friday night," he said.

Todd could feel Grady's stare boring into him as they pulled the raft out of the water. Officer Helgstrom shut the door of the squad car and came walking toward them.

"Now tell me, what were you two doing on the island? Running from more burglars?"

Kevin just shifted his weight from one foot to another. Summoning all his courage, Todd looked Grady straight in the eye. "We think the stolen items from Friday night are on the island."

"What?" roared Grady.

"Why do you think that?" asked Officer Helgstrom, before her partner could continue.

"Yesterday when we were on the bridge we saw something reflecting sunlight," answered Todd. Did he dare tell them about the computer sheet?

"And you two, being the fine upstanding citizens you are, decided to go and investigate," said Grady.

"Yes," replied Todd.

"Did you find the stolen items?" asked Helgstrom.

"No," said Todd, lowering his gaze. "You stopped us before we could finish, but I—"

"Damn right, we stopped you," said Grady, interrupting him. "Do you boys know how much other crap is going on in this area?" He took a step toward them. "Well, do you?"

Todd resisted the urge to take a step backward.

"While you're out worrying your parents sick or trespassing on an island, there have been real burglaries, robberies, and God knows how many drug deals. Yet, we have to spend our overtime baby-sitting you two."

Todd didn't know what to say to defend himself. Grady was convinced they were lying, and nothing but hard evidence would change his mind.

"Who are you?" boomed Grady, as Sam joined them.

"I—I'm his brother," said Sam, pointing to Kevin.

Todd was glad he wasn't the only one Grady scared.

"Well, I hope you can talk some sense into these two. I've got a good mind to take them to the station."

"I'll take them home," said Sam.

"Good." Grady turned to them. "If I so much as see you two near that island again, I'll haul both of you to juvenile hall so fast it'll make your heads spin." He turned around and stomped away.

Helgstrom studied them a moment, then wrote something on a sheet of paper. "If you two have any evidence that would convince me the stuff is out there"—she pointed to the island—"you call me." She handed Todd the paper, and he slipped it into his pocket.

As she started to walk away, confusion clouded Kevin's face. "Aren't you going to tell her—"

Todd shot him a look, and he stopped. Officer Helgstrom turned around. Todd avoided her gaze by pretending to be interested in tipping a rock over with his shoe. Out of the corner of his eye, he saw her shrug her shoulders, then get in the police car.

"Boy, did we luck out," said Kevin, when the car pulled away.

Sam whistled. "That guy looks like he used to be an all-pro linebacker." He turned to them. "You two owe me one for getting you out of this." He paused. "Didn't find anything, did you?"

"Not what we expected," answered Todd.

"Sounds like you were wrong about the stuff," said Sam. Todd didn't answer. "I'm glad you're done. If we hurry home, I can still get another couple hours of sleep." He walked back to the car.

"How come you didn't tell Helgstrom about the computer sheet?" asked Kevin.

"With Grady around?"

Kevin nodded. "I see your point."

"Besides, you heard her. We need evidence before she'll even believe us." He felt for the computer sheet in his shirt pocket. "Right now all we have is a lot of unanswered questions."

Chapter Ten

After agreeing with Kevin to meet at the shopping center at ten o'clock and look at the pictures, Todd went home. He hoped they had turned out, even though he wasn't sure how much help they would be in proving anything. He swerved up the driveway, leaned his bike against the back wall, then breezed into the kitchen.

Jan jumped, knocking her cup over. "You scared me!" She righted the cup and wiped at the spilled tea on her blouse. "I thought you'd still be in bed since there wasn't any school today."

"I went for a ride," he said, opening the refrigerator.

She grabbed a paper towel and dabbed at the stain. "The next time you go for an early morning ride, I'd appreciate you letting me know."

Not this again, thought Todd. He slammed the refrigerator door shut.

"I know, I know," she said. "You think I'm just nagging at you, but I'm not. You really did scare me."

Todd poured a glass of milk.

Jan stopped wiping at the stain and studied him. "I guess I should explain. A few years ago I was living on the first floor of an apartment building. I was in the kitchen eating breakfast, and when I went back to my bedroom there was a man with a knife in his hand standing beside my bedroom window. He'd cut the screen and climbed in."

"So what did you do?" asked Todd, trying not to be too interested.

"I was lucky," she said. "On my right was my dresser and on top of it all my personal toiletries; deodorant, nail polish, a can of hair mousse, that kind of stuff. Well, I started yelling and throwing everything I could get my hands on. I aimed for his face and head and threw as hard and fast as I could. To protect himself, he put his arms up and after a few hits he dropped the knife."

"Then what?"

"He dropped his arms and started for the window. That's when I nailed him with a box of powder. Got him right here." She pointed to a spot on her left cheek. "Powder went everywhere, his face, his clothes, my bed." She rolled her eyes and shook her head.

"What a mess! Anyway he started coughing and sneezing like crazy. He lunged for the window and fell onto the ground outside, then he stumbled off down the alley."

"That really happened?" asked Todd.

"Yes," she answered. "I'll tell you I was never so glad I had been a basketball player and one that could shoot on top of it."

"What happened next?"

"I called the police, and they found him a

few blocks away. Cuts and bruises on his face, powder all over, and a broken arm from falling out the window."

"You're putting me on," said Todd, narrowing his eyes.

"It's true." She raised her hand. "Honest to God."

"Bet he didn't rob anyone for a while." Todd smiled as he pictured the guy skulking down the alley, clutching his arm, and looking like a ghost.

"You think it's funny?" asked Jan.

"I was thinking how ridiculous the guy must've looked," said Todd.

She was silent a moment, then a smile appeared on her lips. "You're right, he did look comical now that I think about it." She dabbed at the stain again. "I told you all of this so that you'd understand I wasn't nagging at you. I thought you were still in bed, and I panicked when I didn't know who was coming in the door."

"I think I understand," said Todd.

Jan looked at the clock. "I'd better hustle and change if I don't want to be late for work."

Todd took a sip of milk as he watched her hurry out. The sharp clicks from her high-heeled shoes stopped when she reached the carpet.

That was quite a story, he thought. Perhaps the fear he'd felt Friday and Sunday nights was the same kind of fear she had felt when she saw the burglar. If it was, he had to give her a lot of credit.

A few minutes later she returned wearing a new outfit. "I'll see you tonight," she said. "Thanks for trying to understand." After giving him a quick pat on the shoulder, she disappeared into the garage.

Up in his bedroom, Todd pushed everything on his dresser to one side and laid out the computer sheet. Dreams Are Yours Vacations was printed in the upper left corner along with the time and date the computer had printed it. Below that were four columns. The first one contained names of people and the second one gave their addresses. Most of the people lived in Winnipeg, Manitoba, with a handful from Duluth, Minnesota. The third column had two letters following each address. There were four different sets: CD, MP, LG, and CH. Were they some kind of identifying code? Perhaps they were people's initials.

In the last column, over half of the money amounts were the one hundred eighty-nine dollar figure—the membership fee Baldy had asked for over the phone. The other amounts ranged from two hundred nineteen dollars to seven hundred fifty-nine dollars.

Todd fetched the small calculator from his dad's desk and added the amounts. He whistled softly. Thirty people in one day had paid eight thousand ninety-three dollars to Dreams Are Yours Vacations. In five days, it added up to over forty thousand dollars. No wonder Baldy didn't want the cops nosing around, thought Todd. Could this somehow be tied in with the burglary? He studied the sheet again. If there was a connection, he couldn't see it.

The paper was still damp and was beginning to tear in the middle where the creases met. He rummaged through his closet and pulled out a piece of cardboard. Carefully he laid the sheet on it, then taped the edges. In one corner, he taped the postcard to the cardboard, then slid the entire thing under his bed.

* * *

"Sorry I'm late," said Kevin, as he pulled up to the bike rack outside the mall. "Mom decided to put me to work. I had to mow the lawn, sweep the basement, and empty the dishwasher. Good thing I had to meet you, she'd probably have me painting the house next."

As they headed toward the photo store, Todd noticed how much quieter it was than yesterday. It was still early and not many shoppers were out yet. After paying for the photos, the two of them found a bench and sat down.

Todd opened the packet of pictures. The first nine were blank. The tenth one was a picture, but it was too dark to distinguish anything. "This must be the one I took in the woods when Baldy and his wife were standing next to the patio door." The eleventh shot was of the garbage can, but it was blurry. "Baldy was starting to come after me here." One more picture; he hoped it had turned out. The last photograph was clear, and you could easily read the words "stereo receiver" and "VCR" printed on the boxes.

"That proves it," said Kevin.

"No, it doesn't," said Todd, looking around. There were a few more people now.

"Why not?" asked Kevin.

"Baldy could say he bought them for another room in the house. Lots of people have more than one television, why not another VCR or stereo receiver?"

"But the police would know he was lying when they went into the house to check," said Kevin.

"Why would they go into the house? Just because *we* say so?" He glared at his friend.

Kevin slumped back into the bench. "I see what you mean." He was silent a minute. "But how are we going to come up with more evidence?"

Todd tapped the photographs against his other hand as he thought about it. Finally he let out a sigh. "The only thing left to do is to go over to Baldy's house and see if there's something else incriminating."

"Yeah, maybe we'll be lucky and Baldy will have put a sign out saying We're Guilty."

Todd groaned.

"You know what?" asked Kevin.

"What?"

"I wish we were older—then we could disguise ourselves as telephone repairmen, like they do on television. Once we got into the house we could tie Baldy up and inject him with a truth serum."

"But we're not and we can't," snapped Todd.

Kevin looked hurt.

"Sorry," said Todd. "I'm worried our clues are drying up." Then where would they be? They still wouldn't get to use the canoe. "Come on, let's go." He shoved the pictures into the packet. Later he would add them to the other evidence.

Kevin followed Todd as he slowly crept through the woods. He spotted the white siding and crouched lower. They'd have to be careful. Coming in full daylight would make it easier for someone to spot them. They settled down behind a fallen tree, not far from the stump where Todd had hidden on Sunday.

A black Mustang sat parked in the driveway. "They've got company," whispered Todd. "Maybe that will lead somewhere." He checked his watch; it was ten to eleven.

The minutes ticked by. Every so often Kevin's stomach growled. Finally at twelve o'clock the sliding glass door opened and Baldy's wife came out. She was wearing a green bikini and carrying a lounge chair. Placing the chair in a sunny spot, she sat down and began rubbing suntan lotion on. A few moments later she lay down on her stomach. Except for her turning over after twenty minutes and Kevin's stomach reminding Todd how hungry he was getting, everything was quiet.

"I don't think I can stay much longer," whispered Kevin, after his stomach gave a particularly long and loud gurgle.

"I know," whispered Todd. He looked around. "I'm getting hungry, too. Maybe you could go home and bring us back something to eat."

Just then the patio door opened and two men stepped outside. One wore a black baseball cap, and the second one had a reddish beard and carried a mail sack. They walked over to Baldy's wife.

It was them! The burglars! The ones who had wrecked the canoe! Todd scrambled to his knees to get a better look.

"We're going to pick up some lunch at the

Vietnamese place near the post office. Want something?" the man with the cap asked.

"Yes," she answered, swinging her legs over the side of the chair. She stood up, and the three of them walked toward the garage. "I'm not sure what I want to eat," she almost shouted.

Todd frowned. She had spoken as if she wanted someone else to hear her. Someone inside the house?

"Maybe I'll have the vegetables and shrimp," she continued, as loudly as before.

Todd expected the three of them to walk through the garage doorway. Instead, they strolled toward the two boys. Todd froze. He didn't even dare breathe. Any movement from him or the foliage surrounding him, and the two men would be down on them in seconds.

The threesome rounded the corner of the garage. Quickly the man in the black cap pushed Baldy's wife against the white siding and started kissing her. They were only sixty feet away. Kevin's stomach gurgled, then let out a loud growl. Todd darted his eyes toward him. A look of horror crossed Kevin's face, and he grabbed his middle and squeezed.

"Come on, Chuck," said the man with the

beard. "He'll suspect something if he doesn't hear the car start soon."

Chuck pulled away from Baldy's wife. "You're right, Mike." He turned back to her. "We'll come in like before." She nodded. "Don't worry, after tonight it'll be all over." He kissed her again. After he released her, the two men swaggered toward the car. She waved as the Mustang backed down the driveway; then she disappeared into the garage.

Todd collapsed to the ground, his leg muscles aching from the awkward pose he had been holding.

"They're the same ones who chased us, aren't they?" asked Kevin.

"Yes," answered Todd, trying to understand what he had just seen and heard.

"But why would they steal from someone they know?"

Todd remembered the computer printout and the sets of letters in the third column. He was willing to bet CD and MP were Chuck's and Mike's initials. And the mailbag Mike carried probably contained more postcards like the one he had. Now the only question left was, how much of the eight thousand dollars a day did they get?

"I'm pretty sure Chuck and Mike work for Baldy," said Todd. "Maybe they stole from him because he's cheating them out of money."

"Makes sense," said Kevin, nodding his head in agreement. "What do you think the guy meant when he said it would be all over to-night?"

"I'm not sure," answered Todd. "It could mean Chuck and Baldy's wife are running off together or maybe it means they're going to shut down the operation and move somewhere else." He looked at the house. "Whatever it means, I think we have to be here."

Kevin swallowed. "I was afraid you'd say that."

Chapter Eleven

"I was wondering if I'd see you this afternoon," said Dad, when Todd entered the kitchen.

"Kevin and I were out riding around." Todd winced at his partial lie. If only he could tell his father what he'd really been up to, the pictures, the trip to the island, then seeing the two men from Friday night. But if he did, he was sure Dad would tell him to call the police and forbid him to pursue it any further.

He couldn't have that happen. No one believed them yet, except maybe Jan. Everything that could prove their innocence was . . . What did the lawyers on television call it? Circumstantial evidence, that was the term. Perhaps tonight, something would happen to change that.

". . . up north at a cabin for vacation," said Dad. "How does that sound to you?"

"What?" asked Todd.

"I was talking about vacation and the three of us renting a cabin."

"Sounds good," said Todd, trying to keep his mind on the conversation.

"I have to go to the bank, then run a couple of errands so I'm leaving in a few minutes." He paused. "Anything you want to talk to me about?"

"No," answered Todd. From the look on his father's face he realized he'd answered too quickly. "Vacation at a cabin sounds like fun," he added. "We can go fishing."

"Good, I'm glad you agree." Dad rose from the chair.

Todd watched him push it into the table. He had the feeling his dad wanted to say something else, but he just patted the top of the chair, then left.

* * *

It was almost five o'clock when the phone rang. Thinking it was Kevin, Todd raced downstairs to answer it.

"Todd," Jan's voice was at the other end. "I'm stopping at a friend's house for a while. Make yourself a sandwich, and I'll fix us something after I get home."

"Sure," said Todd, grateful for the time alone.

"I should be home about eight o'clock."

"I'm going to meet Kevin at six-thirty," said Todd. "I might stay overnight." There. He'd covered himself in case it started getting too late.

"Thanks for telling me," said Jan. "See you tomorrow. Bye."

Todd put the phone down, then peeked into the cupboards. She was right about eating something, he thought. Who knew how long it might take tonight? He tossed the loaf of bread on the counter and made a sandwich.

At six o'clock he was too nervous to stay home any longer. He jumped on his trusty BMX and sped toward the bridge. Halfway there, he clutched at his shirt pocket—yes, the camera was there.

A few people were on the walking and bicycle paths, but nothing like on the weekend. When he reached the bridge, he spotted thick, dark clouds gathering in the northwest. It looked like rain. No wonder there weren't many people out.

A few minutes later Kevin pulled up to him. "I hope whatever they do tonight, they do it early," he said. "This waiting around is awful."

Kevin's cheeks were red. Todd wondered if it was from the bike ride or from being scared. "Come on," he said. "Let's go."

They set out for Balsam Lake, neither of them saying anything. Todd wished he had more of an idea what might happen tonight. He felt unprepared and scared, just like the night Mom and Dad told him they were getting a divorce. There hadn't been any book to help him then, or now. They dropped their bikes in the usual place, then silently crept to their hiding spot behind the fallen tree.

Nothing appeared to be happening in the house. The drapes on the sliding glass doors were drawn, and there was still too much daylight to see if any indoor lights were turned on. The black Mustang was gone.

"I'm going to check and see if the car is in the garage," said Todd, climbing over the dead tree. His heartbeat quickened as he dodged and darted from tree to tree. At the edge of the lawn he checked the street; it was empty. He dashed across the twenty feet of grass to the side wall of the garage. Slowly he raised his head and peered through the window. Only two things sat inside, the white Audi and the garbage can. He hadn't thought of it before, but now he wondered who cut the grass. Quickly he turned and raced back to Kevin.

"The car's there," he said, when he slid down next to Kevin. "So they haven't left yet, and I bet they've been using a lawn service."

"What?" Kevin looked at him like he'd just said the most absurd thing in the world. "Something important is going to happen and you calmly say they use a lawn service." He shook his head. "Did I miss something?"

"There's no lawn mower," said Todd. "The garage is empty except for the car and a garbage can."

"Whew!" said Kevin. "For a second there you had me worried. I thought you were getting weird on me like the time you tried to jump over that water fountain with your bike and fell off and hit your head."

Todd winced. It had been embarrassing, falling in front of Kevin, Jackson, and Terry. They had teased him for at least a month afterward. He had a concussion and had to stay out of school a few days.

Light rain began to hit the tree canopy. "If it doesn't rain much harder, we should stay dry for a while," said Todd, looking up.

Kevin glanced at his watch. "It's eight-fifteen. Do you think they'll bring in a moving van or something?"

"I don't know," answered Todd. It was starting to get dark enough for him to see light coming through the patio drapes. If he shifted to his right three feet, he could see lights on upstairs. It rained harder and drops fell from the leaves.

"I hope something happens soon," said Kevin, wiping his forehead.

The rain dampened their excitement, and they were silent as they kept watch. Finally, at eight-forty, the drapes were brushed aside, and Baldy's wife stood there, peering outside. She reached a hand to the latch, then pulled on the door. A thin shaft of light escaped to the patio. She looked out again, then let the drapes fall back into place.

"What was that about?" asked Kevin.

Todd didn't answer. The image of Baldy holding the boxes and pointing angrily at the door stuck in his mind. Had she left it open purposely for Chuck and Mike to get in? Was that how they were going to enter tonight?

Kevin grabbed his arm. "Listen."

Todd cocked his head toward the lake, but the rain made it difficult to distinguish sounds. Finally he heard a faint, metallic scrape. Then a few seconds later a twig snapped. He swallowed. Had they been seen? His senses were on full alert. He heard the sound of footsteps. Someone was coming up the path. Squinting, he could see two shadowy figures crouched at the edge of the lawn. Suddenly they straightened and ran toward the house.

In the light from the door, Todd could see it was Chuck and Mike. Silently they slid the patio door open, then slipped inside. Within a few seconds the light from the second-floor window moved, grew brighter, then darker.

"We have to find out what's going on," said Todd, and he jumped over the tree and raced for the garage. He darted to the patio door and strained to hear. Muffled noises came from upstairs, then the sounds and voices grew louder.

"You won't be cheating us anymore," snarled Chuck.

The finality of the statement sent a shiver down Todd's spine.

"But you told me you weren't going to hurt him," she pleaded.

"Did I say that?" asked Chuck.

Todd heard Mike laugh.

"Listen, baby," said Chuck. "When you gave us the code word for Charles's computer program, we were able to see just how much money this bastard's been cheating us out of."

Todd's jaw dropped. They were talking about the computer sheet he had at home!

"The only reason we took the rest of the stuff was to make it look like a burglary so Charles wouldn't hurt you." He paused. "Understand?"

"Yes, but you didn't say anything about . . ." Todd could hear her crying.

The sounds came closer. He bolted for the woods and dived over the tree just as the two men reached the patio door.

Chuck came out first, his back to them. He was hunched over as if carrying something. The bearded man, Mike, followed. When they turned toward the lake, Todd gasped. They were carrying a body! Baldy's limp form lay motionless in their arms.

"We'll finish him off on the island," said Chuck to the woman. "Start packing—you're moving in with us."

Baldy's wife nodded her head, then stepped back into the house. The two men headed for the path and within seconds were swallowed up by the darkness. A couple of minutes later a scraping noise drifted up from the lake.

Todd sat there stunned. Had he really seen this? This was murder! His heart pounded in his chest.

"Wh-what do we do now?" asked Kevin.

Todd heard the disbelief in his friend's voice. His mind darted in all directions. They had to do something. Let somebody know. Let the police know. "Polaski!" he blurted out.

He jumped to his feet and raced for Huron Street. The lights were on at Burt's house. He flew up the steps and began jabbing the doorbell.

"Okay! Okay! Hold your horses. I'm coming," said Mr. Polaski irritably. Todd could hear his grumbling through an open window. Kevin came up behind him. "And what is so all fire important that you have to ring the doorbell to death?" asked Burt, opening the door.

"It's me, Todd Benson. Remember? My dad and I stopped by Saturday. You have to call the police. Baldy's going to be killed on Sanctuary Island!"

"Whoa boys," said Burt, putting his hands up. "What's this all about? Who's Baldy?"

"The guy in the house up there," pointed Todd. "He's running a scam, and the two guys who work for him have just beaten him up."

Burt stroked his chin. "I think you boys had better come inside and explain this. It'll give you a chance to dry off some." He reached for them.

"There isn't time!" yelled Todd. He backed down the steps. "Just call the police and tell them to go to Sanctuary Island." He turned and bolted across the grass.

"Wait!" called Burt, but the boys were gone.

"We have to keep track of them somehow," said Todd, slowing enough to let Kevin catch up. "We have to make sure they don't toss Baldy overboard before they reach the island."

"We'll be able to see them from the Lakewood Drive bridge," panted Kevin.

"Yeah, you're right," said Todd.

They dragged their bikes from the hiding spot. Todd figured it would take the canoe at least twenty-five minutes to get to the bridge. Five minutes had passed already. If they hurried, they would make it.

The rain felt like needles hitting Todd's face as they careened around the curve leading to the bridge. Two streetlights bathed the bridge in a yellowish haze. Shoot! He'd forgotten about them. If they stood on the bridge, the two men would see them. They'd have to go down the embankment on the other side and watch from there.

They raced across the bridge and immediately Todd slammed on his brakes. He leaped off and pushed the bike down the hill, letting it crash to the ground when he reached the lilac bushes. Swiftly he crawled around the maze of tangled stems. Kevin followed, his labored breathing letting Todd know how far behind he was. Todd stopped when he could see the streetlight's reflection on the water.

"How long before they come through?" asked Kevin.

"Maybe five minutes," answered Todd.

A car sped over the bridge, the whine from its tires fading as it drove away. It was only the third car they'd seen tonight, thought Todd. He wiped the sweat and rain away from his forehead. The foul weather was keeping people away from the lakes. Chuck and Mike couldn't have picked a better night to commit murder.

Suddenly he heard something. There it was, again, and again. The faint gurgle of water rushing in to fill the space left by the paddle. It had to be them. The bow slid into view. Quickly the canoe glided over the water, just catching the edge of the reflection from the streetlight.

Todd spotted a tarp-covered bundle in front of the center thwart. Good. They still had Baldy. The canoe vanished into the darkness, and the soft sounds faded.

"Let's go," whispered Todd.

"Why aren't the cops showing up?" asked Kevin.

"I don't know." Todd was getting worried. When they reached the path, he scanned the lake for flashing lights. "They should be here by now." Everything hinged on the fact that the police would show up. If they didn't come soon, it would be too late!

Part of a plan began to form in his mind. "Come on," he said hastily. "We have to get to my place."

Minutes later they pulled up next to the outside garage wall.

"Wait!" cried Kevin. He tripped over his bike. "What are we doing?"

"We're going to take the canoe out on the lake and leave Chuck and Mike stranded on the island."

"What?"

"Sssh," said Todd, looking at the light coming through the kitchen window. "If Jan hears us she won't let us go." Kevin nodded. "We'll carry the canoe like we did before."

"But what about the hole?" asked Kevin.

"We made it from Balsam Lake on Friday night. We should be able to make it out to Sanctuary Island and back again. Hurry!"

Kevin ducked under the bow and raised the canoe with his shoulder. Todd did the same with the stern. "Grab a paddle on the way out," he whispered, as loud as he dared. Through the kitchen door window he caught a glimpse of Jan. She was talking on the telephone.

They half ran, half stumbled their way toward the lake. When they reached the bicycle path, Todd heard the geese on the island making a racket. He hoped that meant Chuck and Mike had just gotten there. Now the question was, how long would it take them to finish off Baldy and hide the body?

They staggered into the shallows and clumsily turned the canoe right side up. Kevin climbed in first, then Todd pushed them away from shore. Cold water squished inside his tennis shoes, and his hands shook as he gripped the paddle.

They paddled swiftly, making as little noise as possible. Todd decided they would approach the island the same way they had this morning. He was gambling that the two men had put in somewhere near there.

As they drew closer to the island, Todd used his shirtsleeve to wipe away the rain from his eyes. He didn't want anything blocking his vision.

"There it is," whispered Kevin.

"I don't see it,"

"It's on the left, fifty feet ahead." Kevin pointed with his paddle.

Todd strained to see the canoe. A form appeared at the water line. Another few feet—yes, now he could see it clearly. Quickly he angled the paddle so that the stern of their canoe floated toward the stern of the second canoe. The two craft inched toward each other. Todd slipped the paddle from the water and silently laid it in the canoe. He didn't dare risk another dropped paddle, not this close to two murderers.

His left hand reached for the canoe. It swayed slightly under the pressure. Todd figured at least the rear third of it was still in the water. Using his right hand, he searched the bang plate for a tie-off rope.

"Hurry," urged Kevin. Todd could barely hear him.

Three inches down, a rope was tied to the towing link. He picked up both ends and tied them together, then he slipped his leg through the newly made loop and brought the knot up so that it was just above his knee.

"Go!" he whispered.

They stabbed at the water with their paddles. The canoe lunged forward. The rope grew taut, yanking Todd's knee against the gunwale. Their forward momentum stopped. Todd winced at the throbbing in his leg. They kept paddling. The canoe lurched forward. Slowly a loud scraping noise filled the air as the second canoe was dragged off the shore.

"What the hell!" shouted a voice in the woods. Branches cracked. Footsteps thundered toward them.

The towed canoe was fifteen feet from shore

when Todd heard the first splash. He whipped his head around. A second splash broke the lake's dark surface.

"They coming after us!" yelled Todd. He stabbed at the water. Twenty-five feet. He couldn't let them latch onto their canoe! Forty feet. They would jerk him overboard. Sixty feet. He didn't want to die!

"God, I swear I'll never sneak another doughnut if you'll just get us out of this!" yelled Kevin.

Police sirens screamed in the distance. Todd prayed they were coming toward the lake. Just then two squad cars, a fire truck, and a van with trailer rounded the curve at the south end of the lake. Within a couple of minutes, a boat with spotlights raced toward them. It slowed, pulling within twenty feet. Sheriff's Department Water Patrol was printed on the side.

"There're two guys in the water near the island! They've killed a third man and he's on the island!" yelled Todd.

The boat with three officers and a paramedic pulled away. Todd held onto the gunwales as waves rocked the canoes. The spotlights illuminated the island and the two men as they climbed out of the water.

"All right!" said Kevin. "Now they look like the sewer rats they are. Serves them right."

Todd grinned. "We did it! Now everyone will have to believe us." He watched the officers frisk the two men. Finally it was all over. They had outwitted the bad guys. "Come on, let's head in."

They paddled toward the flashing red lights. Todd was glad when they reached shore. Not only did his knee hurt where it had banged against the gunwale, but the rope was starting to cut into the soft, fleshy area on the inside of his leg. Two officers they didn't know helped them pull the canoes onto shore.

Jan appeared, carrying a couple of blankets. "This is getting to be a habit with you two." She handed one to each of them.

"Thanks," said Todd. Now that his adrenaline had stopped pumping, he felt cold. He wrapped the blanket around himself. An ambulance and a third squad car pulled up. Officers Helgstrom and Grady stepped out of the car.

"You want to tell us what's going on?" asked Helgstrom.

Todd looked at Grady, but the big man remained quiet. "The two guys out there, they're the same ones from Friday night. They work for the third man."

"We call him Baldy," interrupted Kevin.

"Right," continued Todd. "They're running a vacation scam operation out of the house on Huron Street. Baldy's been cheating the other two so they decided to get rid of him."

"The wife is in on it, too," said Kevin.

"I see," said Helgstrom.

"He's got pictures and a computer printout," added Kevin.

"Wonderful." She turned to her partner. "I'll put a call in to have the wife picked up. Grady, don't you have something to say to these two?"

Grady was silent a moment. "Good job," he said gruffly, then he turned on his heel and marched away.

Todd looked at Kevin. "Did I hear what I think I heard?"

"Yeah," answered Kevin. "Hey, maybe our names will be in the papers tomorrow."

Just then the boat pulled up to shore and they watched the officers lift a stretcher over the side, then carry it to the ambulance. Next the two men were helped onto the ground. Handcuffed, they were led to a squad car.

"Is he dead?" Todd heard Grady ask the paramedic.

"Blow to the head, pulse is weak, hard to say if he'll make it," answered the man.

Todd was glad Baldy wasn't dead. If he pulled through, he could testify against the other two.

Two cars drove up as the ambulance sped away. Todd's dad jumped out of one and Kevin's mother and Sam scrambled out of the other.

"Todd!" His father sprinted toward him. "You better have a good reason for scaring me to death!"

"They do," said Officer Helgstrom, coming up behind him. "They've probably prevented a murder and helped us shut down an entire vacation scam operation."

"What?" His father stood there with his mouth open looking at the boys, then at Helgstrom.

"We'll need a statement from you two," she said. "We're going to send the boat back out and look for the stolen property. Perhaps you could go home, change into some dry clothes, then come down to the station. Bring your evidence, too."

"We will," said Todd. Suddenly he felt very tired.

Officer Helgstrom turned to Jan. "Good thing you called when you did. A few more minutes and that guy would have been a goner." She looked at the boys. "See you at the station." With that, she left.

"You called?" Todd was confused.

"Mr. Polaski called the house looking for your father. He told me what you said. You must've come and taken the canoe when I was on the phone with him. I called Helgstrom, and she put it together about the island. Then I called your dad and Kevin's mother."

"I think we'd better get these two dried off," said Mrs. Jarvis, putting an arm around Kevin.

"We can't forget the canoe," said Todd.

His dad looked at him. "After all that's happened you're still worrying about that canoe." He shook his head. "I think it's time I reversed my decision. You two can use the canoe this summer. I'll try and fix it this weekend."

"All right!" said Todd, beaming.

"I don't have any rope along," said Dad. "Jan, would you help me put the canoe in the car? I'll open the hatch, and we'll slide it inside."

"Guess I'll have to clean my own car since my little brother's such a hotshot detective," said Sam.

"Yeah, Kevin and Todd, teen detectives. We're going to be famous. People from around the world will call and ask for our help." Kevin declared. "We might even let you help on our next case."

Sam shoved him playfully. "You better tell me how you figured all this out."

Mrs. Jarvis began steering Kevin toward the car. He was still chattering when he managed to wriggle his hand out from under the blanket and give Todd a thumbs-up sign.

"Looks like you're riding with me," Jan said, when she came back from helping Dad. They got into the car, and she started it up.

"Uh—thanks for calling the cops," said Todd.

"You're welcome," said Jan. "By the way, your dad mentioned something about the three of us spending our vacation at a cabin." She paused a few seconds. "I was wondering if some evening you would be willing to teach me how to fish?"

"Only if *I* make the sandwiches," said Todd, grinning.

"Deal," said Jan, and they headed home.

A. M. MONSON

spent her childhood years on a Wisconsin farm. She attended first grade in a one-room schoolhouse, played hide-and-seek with her dog in the cornfields, spun stories in the cow pasture. Now living in Minneapolis, where she works as a city bus driver and writes, she has never lost her love of the outdoors. She canoes and camps, hikes and crosscountry skiis, and is currently saving her money for a wind surfer to take out on Lake Superior.

Speaking about her inspiration for this book, Ms. Monson says, "Many times when we're growing up, there are things that happen that are totally out of our control. It's as if everyone else—parents, teachers, even siblings and friends—has power over us. When I was thirteen, I was a little like Todd in this book. I longed for some of that power, longed to prove once in a while that *I* was right."